Kentucky

MW01264552

Copyright © 2017 by R. David Anderson

All rights reserved. No part of this publication may be reproduced, distributed, or transmitted in any form or by any means, including photocopying, recording, or other electronic or mechanical methods, without the prior written permission of the publisher, except in the case of brief quotations embodied in critical reviews and certain other noncommercial uses permitted by copyright law.

This is a work of fiction. Names, characters, businesses, places, events and incidents are either the products of the author's imagination or used in a fictitious manner. Any resemblance to actual persons, living or dead, or actual events is purely coincidental.

Index

The Terrible Storm

A brisk autumn wind rustled through the trees, blowing leaves across my backyard. I love Kentucky this time of year when the trees change color with the fall season. The woods near my house glimmered in the late afternoon sunshine.

A weekend storm was in the forecast, and dark clouds moved in from the south.

This house has weathered many a bad storm. In my 68 years, I have also weathered a few. I was alone in the house now. My husband of 43 years passed away last June. I would weather this storm alone.

I made myself a cup of hot tea and sat at the dining room table. My dog Muffin, a golden retriever, snuggled at my feet. She's my constant companion, I feel safe with her by my side. But I know that Muffin is afraid of thunder, and the storm is getting close. The lights flickered.

Every few seconds there was a flash of lightening and the windows were shaking from the thunder. Muffin whined and snuggled closer to my feet. I looked out the window at the trees bending back and forth in the strong winds. I was fearful that one might fall on my house.

I heard a horse outside. It sounded frightened and was crying out in loud panic-stricken shrieks. The horse galloped up the gravel lane towards the house, then ran into my back yard. There was a bright lightening flash as the brown male quarter horse reared up on its hind legs and once again let out a loud piercing cry. Muffin ran for the back bedroom in fear.

I ran out the back door, hoping to somehow corral the horse at the barn yard. It continued to romp back on its hind legs, ranting.

I gently spoke to the to the frightened horse. "It's okay, don't be afraid. I'm here to help you."

The beautiful horse looked at me for a moment. I walked slowly towards him.

"Don't be afraid, boy. I am here."

There was another flash of lightening, and the horse bolted towards the woods. I watched as he ran at full speed through some low brush in a field.

He was gone. I blinked my eyes in disbelief. The horse had just vanished! I shook my head. It was as though the horse had not been there.

Heavy sheets of rain began to fall, so I retreated back to the house. I dried off, then poured myself some more hot tea and sat down. Muffin came out of hiding and stayed by my side.

The lights flickered on and off again. I got up and pulled some candles and a pocket flashlight from a drawer. I was going to be ready in case the power went out.

I could not get the terrified horse out of my mind. I was trying to remember if any of my neighbors had horses. I had not seen this horse before; he may have been from a farm from the Mint Spring area.

The storm was worsening. Winds were whipping the trees into a frenzy, and lightening followed with deafening bursts of thunder. This would make it worse for the poor frightened horse. A spooked horse could run for miles and quickly become lost.

Then again, the horse seemed to vanish. That was very strange. Perhaps my vision was getting worse. Time to have my eyes checked.

I looked out the window; it was now pouring down in sheets. Daylight had faded away completely. The winds were howling around the house in a relentless tempest. The lights flickered on and off again, then they went out completely. The house was now in pitch darkness.

A burst of wind blew open the back door. A strong gust swished through the living room, knocking off some books from a wall shelf. I rushed over and closed the door and locked it. Then I grabbed the flashlight and picked up the mess on the floor. That's when I saw a familiar book that I had not seen in many years. It was Ginny's journal.

I had shelved the journal thirty years earlier and forgotten where it was. I was happy to have discovered it again.

I returned to the dining table and put the journal there, lit a candle, and sat down. Muffin came back to snuggle at my feet.

The storm continued to rage outside, and winds whipped and howled around the house like some kind of demon. The flicker of the candle brought a warm glow to the room.

I picked up the journal and blew the dust from the worn, brown cover. A yellowed sheet of paper fell out onto the table. I recognized what it was immediately. It was a family tree that I had drawn up a long time ago, when I had traced my lineage back to Ginny Chamberlain's time; my great-great step grandmother.

I studied the sheet of paper. I recalled how Ginny and Pelina had been best friends, growing up in rural Jefferson County near Harrods Creek. Pelina had two daughters, Kate and Sarah. Ginny had raised the two girls after Pelina had died from a long illness in 1889. Kate was my great grandmother, and her daughter, Clara, my grandmother. Here is the family tree that I traced:

My Family Tree:
1850 Ginny Chamberlain born on a farm outside Louisville, Kentucky
1874 Kate born (Pelina's daughter, Ginny's stepdaughter)
1896 Clara born (daughter of Kate)

1920 My Mother born (daughter of Clara)

1950 I am born

The journal had been in my possession for a year or so when I drew up this lineage in 1971. That was forty-seven years ago. I had found it in 1970, forty-eight years ago. My Grandmother Beason (Clara) died that year.

It had been many years since I had read Ginny's journal. I opened the front cover. On the first page written in neat cursive lettering with blue ink from a fountain pen was my great-great step grandmother's name. The page was yellowed and brittle, smelled dirty, yet the lettering of the name was exceptionally clear.

I turned the page. The candle was not sufficient light to read by with my poor vision. I needed a better light source. There was a battery-operated hurricane lamp somewhere up in the cabinet above the refrigerator. I grabbed a foot stool and looked for it with my flashlight. I found the light almost towards the rear of the cabinet. I could barely reach it. I got it down and flicked the switch to the "on" position. The batteries were dead. Fortunately, I had new batteries in a utensil drawer. I replaced the batteries and turned it on. A soft glow radiated throughout the room. It was now possible to read with this better light source. I could read the journal for as long as the batteries lasted in the hurricane lamp.

I always called it a journal, but there were over one hundred hand written pages within the tattered covers. It was actually a memoir, containing many details of Ginny's recollections.

Yes, I had found the journal in 1970. I can remember that day clearly. I was 20 years old, and my Grandmother Beason had died that spring. Her house, near Story Avenue in Louisville, had been locked up and unoccupied for over a month. My Mother had decided to sell off everything in an estate sale and prepare the house to be shown by a realtor.

We arrived at the house by mid-morning on a Saturday, the second week of June. Mother had problems opening the door. Her key turned the lock, but the door was jammed. She threw her body weight against the door and put out her shoulder. An old man from the house next door came and helped us to get in with a crow bar. The police came, and my Mother had to explain to them what we were doing there.

The house smelled musty inside and was dark. All the utilities were off. We took inventory of the items that were going to be in the estate sale, noting the things we would keep. Then we went up to the attic where grandmother had many things in storage.

There were some windows in the attic, so it was possible to see all the clutter on the floor. Boxes of toys, magazines, and clothing were strewn about. I bumped against something, then a large doll fell onto the floor in front of me as I walked by. Its eyes seemed to be fixed on mine. My Mother sensed my anxiety and she placed the doll back onto a box of toys.

There were two large wooden trunks in front of us with curved tops and ornate metallic framework. Neither chest was locked. Mother pulled the latch up on one of the trunks and opened a squeaky lid. There were all sorts of items stuffed inside, and the contents appeared to be ancient. The second trunk was also crammed with old stuff.

Mother sorted through one trunk and I rummaged through the other. Mother found a wedding dress and some ladies hats and shoes. There was a beautiful hand stitched quilt in the trunk I was going through. Mother let out a long "aaahhhh" when she saw it.

Under the quilt there were some games and children's clothing, old books, and to my surprise, an old revolver in a holster belt. Mother gasped when she saw it.

"There's a gun!" I exclaimed.

"Let me see that!" Mother cried with a look of disbelief in her eyes. She examined it closely.

"I think that this is over one hundred years old!"

I watched Mother as she pulled the gun from the holster and looked at it from every angle.

"I hope it's not loaded," she said with a very worried look. "Stand back!"

She pointed the gun up at a rafter and pulled the hammer slowly back and pressed the trigger. The firearm clicked. No bullets in the gun.

Mother returned the gun to its holster and we continued to rummage through the trunks. At the bottom of my trunk I found some old documents, land deeds, letters, and Ginny's journal.

I opened the journal and we skimmed through some of the pages. The earliest entries were made prior to 1865, and many of the events described took place around the time of the Civil War.

We returned all the items back to the trunks and then carried them down to our Ford van. Believe me that was a lot of work carrying those heavy trunks down the stairs and lifting them into the van.

We finished up our work at the house just in time for lunch. Everything was ready for the estate sale next weekend.

Once we arrived at our house in Prospect, we carried the trunks to the garage. I pulled out Ginny's journal right away. I was excited to read it to learn more about my great-great step grandmother.

I took the journal to my room and read it many times during the summer of 1970. I was not enrolled in any classes at the University over the summer, so I had plenty of time to comb through the pages.

I slipped backwards in time as I read; to events that had happened in the mid-19th century. I became immersed in the day to day life of my great-great grandmother.

I was young then, now I am old, and once again slipping backwards in time.

Ginny's Journal

Here are Ginny's writings which I have pieced together from her journal and letters which we found in the trunk from my grandmother's house on Story Avenue. I had enough sources to put together a small book. Here is her story.

My Early Memories

My full name was Virginia, but everyone always called me Ginny.

I was born and raised on a farm near Louisville, Kentucky in 1850. My father knew how to breed horses, so when he came to Kentucky, he bought some land and began a horse farm. We had some of the best thoroughbreds in the area, and our horses were in high demand regionally.

A winding dirt lane went from the main pike up to our house. We would travel up and down the dusty lane in our horse drawn carriage. The carriage even had a canopy cover. There was a stone bridge that spanned a creek near a bend in the road. Beyond this, there were wide open green pastures interspersed with wooded areas. A strong wood rail fence went all the way up towards our house, which was surrounded by some tall oak trees.

We lived in a two-story log farm house. I think that the house was there before we purchased the land, because it appeared to have been built several years earlier. It was built of squared timbers, with a long front porch. There were three rooms on the first floor: a kitchen, a combined dining - living room with an enormous fire place made of roughhewn stone, and a simple parlor.

Up on the second floor there was just one long room, with stairs in the middle and two windows on either end. It was an attic room; the shape of the roof defined the inner spaces. There was a wooden railing where the stairs came up, but otherwise the room was wide open, and we all slept up there. The space was partitioned with tall chest-of-drawers. The beds were good. It was comfortable even on cold winter nights, snuggled in a quilt and bed sheets, the fire sending its warmth upwards from below through the wide floor boards.

In the evening father would come in from the fields with his brothers and farm hands, and they would sit down at the long wooden table that was in the center of the main room. The fire was roaring, and tonight mother was cooking a rabbit stew and biscuits. She wore a long ankle length dress; grey, straps over the shoulders, and a bonnet. She was an attractive, slim woman with medium length blonde hair.

She stirred the stew. I brought the bowls and she filled them, then I took them and served the men. Mother also had warm bread from the brick oven. The men talked and laughed as they downed the hearty meal. After the men were served, I sat down in my chair and ate my portion and listened to the men talk.

My mother was a hard-working woman, very serious, with an occasional smile. She had emigrated to this country from Germany as a little girl. Father was clean shaven with short brown hair. He was a strong self-made individual who never tired of his constant labors, and he had made our farm the envy of the county.

August was a busy time on our farm. I was out of school in the summer time, so I had many chores to do. I was expected to rise early in the morning, and Mama woke me up on this particular morning rattling her pans down in the kitchen. I laid back in my bed waiting for her to call me. Soon I could smell breakfast cooking.

"Ginny! It's time to get up!" Mother shouted from the bottom of the stairs.

"Yes, Mama!" I got up and put on a flowery purple cotton blouse, then a cream-colored smock and a simple gathered skirt.

My entire wardrobe was very simple. I usually wore long cotton dresses with a bonnet. My fancy dresses were made of a very silky material, and I usually wore these only when I went to a special occasion; like church, or to town. I only had two fancy dresses. My everyday dresses were of cotton with plaid or floral patterns. I had one favorite dress that was green plaid, and I wore a white bonnet with it.

I laced up an old pair of high top shoes, affixed a white ribbon in my curly brown hair, then ran downstairs to the kitchen.

The sweet aroma of cinnamon pastries filled the kitchen. Mama was using her new wood stove to bake. My little brother Andrew raced down the stairs wearing faded overalls, blue shirt and suspenders.

Pastries were a treat, and that made this a very special morning. My mouth was watering as Mama took them out of the oven. Andrew's eyes nearly popped out of his head as she placed the pastries on the table. Mama put some butter in a crockery dish and set it on the table.

Papa came in with a pail of milk, and he poured it into a porcelain milk pitcher. Then he sat at the head of the table as Mama gave him some hot coffee.

"Going to the fields after breakfast to look at the corn," Papa said, clearing his throat.

Mama nodded. "Bring some for the table, it will go good with dinner."

"The pastries are delicious," Papa said.

"My recipe is from the Old World," Mama smiled.

Papa ate two pastries and slurped down his coffee.

There was a knock at the back door. "Come in!" Papa shouted.

Uncle Jed came in.

"Sit down, Jed. Have some coffee and pastries," Papa said.

Jed sat down, and Mama poured him some hot coffee as he took a pastry from the plate.

"Gonna' hunt tonight and break in a new hound," Jed said.

Papa chuckled. "You gettin' anything on those hunts?"

"Not much. Coon, rabbit, and ran into a skunk the other night."

Papa laughed. "That right? They can make a stink worse than an outhouse. Think I'll pass this time."

Papa and Uncle Jed finished breakfast and went down to the stables to harness the draft horse.

I helped Mama clear the table.

"The slop bucket is full," Mama said. "Go and slop the pigs."

I went out to the back porch to get the slop bucket. It was running over with food waste. I picked it up and headed for the pig sty. I threw the slop into the feeding trough. The pigs scurried over and ate ravenously.

I saw my goats and lambs in the barnyard. I had to go see Miss Muffin, my favorite goat.

I climbed over the wood rail fence and as soon as I was inside the barnyard the goats walked towards me, Miss Muffin leading the pack. I hugged Miss Muffin around her soft muzzle as she licked my ear.

"Oh, Miss Muffin, you look so lovely today! Are you glad to see me?"

I picked some leaves from a nearby maple tree and watched as she chomped them in her mouth. I patted her back as she ate.

I could hear voices coming from the back of the barn. Father and Uncle Jed were busy hitching up the draft horse. I went into the barn and there were Thunder, Breeze and Missy in their stalls. I gave them each a handful of hay. They neighed softly and scraped their front hoofs on the ground. I gave them more hay and hugged their muzzles.

Papa came into the barn to get something. He grabbed some reins.

"Ginny, you makin' over those horses again? You should be in the kitchen helpin' your ma!"

"Papa, is it okay if I go with you and Uncle Jed to the corn fields?"

"Hmm...well..." he stammered. "Go ask your Ma. If she says yes, you can go."

I ran excitedly back to the house. Ma had her wash pan out and she was washing dishes.

"Ginny! What in heavens' name took you so long to slop those pigs? And where's my slop bucket?"

"Sorry, Mama. I'll go fetch it right now."

I ran back to the pig sty and grabbed the slop bucket, then ran back to the house at full steam and put the bucket where it belonged on the porch. I glanced towards the barn. It looked like Papa and Uncle Jed were about to go. I ran back into the kitchen.

"Mama, may I go with Papa and Uncle Jed to the corn field?"

"You have house chores to do, Ginny. You'll just get all dirty and I'll have more dirt to clean up."

"Please, Mama. I promise that I'll do all my house chores when I get back."

Mama was silent. "You dry these dishes, then I might think about it."

I dried the dishes quickly and put them away. Then I grabbed a broom and swept the kitchen floor for good measure, hoping that would persuade Mama to let me go.

I glanced out the window. Papa and Uncle Jed were finished hitching up the draft horse to the hay wagon. They were about to leave without me.

"Mama! Papa and Uncle Jed are leaving! I'm gonna get left behind!"

Mama looked out the window. "Okay, Ginny, you're excused. Remember to bring me some corn for the table tonight."

I propped the broom into the corner and dashed out the door. I was excited to go with Papa and Uncle Jed, and to be free from my chores for once.

Jed sat up on the driver's bench seat. I hopped up onto the back of the hay wagon just as he shook the reins and sounded out two rapid tongue clickers to signal the horse to go. The horse moved forward at a steady pace. Papa came from the barn with a stack of bushel baskets which he placed on the wagon. He walked to the barnyard gate and opened it wide, closing it once we had cleared the corral area.

We traversed open pasture towards the corn field. Once we reached the corn, Uncle Jed slowed the wagon to a crawl, while Papa entered the field, squeezing the green plump ears to see if the crop was ready.

About halfway up the field I jumped down from the wagon onto the dusty, rutted lane, worn by years of wagon wheel impressions in the ground. I walked behind the wagon for a ways, then I ran behind Papa.

"Mama said to pick some corn for dinner!" I blurted.

"There's some good ears in here, "Papa smiled. "Let's get the bushel baskets and pick some for the table."

I followed Papa, holding the bushel basket. He squeezed many ears, picking the ripe ones. The basket filled quickly.

Papa showed me how to pick an ear of ripe corn. I looked for ears with dark brown silk, and then I squeezed the ear to check the plumpness of the kernels. I was proud to have picked many "ready" ears of corn for Papa. We had two bushels filled for the table in no time.

I was about to pick another ear when Papa said, "that's enough for now." As I pulled away from the stalk, a corn leaf swung upwards and hit my left ear. I heard a buzzing and felt the vibration of an insect near my ear opening, then a sharp pain. I cried out in agony, holding my ear.

Papa rushed over and looked at my throbbing ear. He picked me up and walked back to the wagon.

"What's the matter?" Uncle Jed asked.

"She's been stung on her ear by a yellow jacket," Papa answered.

He put me back on the hay wagon, loaded the corn, and we headed back to the house.

My ear was still stinging when we were back in the kitchen. Mama put some soothing salve on the sting.

After the bee sting incident, I continued to help Pa out in the fields. I especially liked helping him with the animals. I loved being with the horses, goats and lambs. When I was in the barnyard Miss Muffin and a pack of goats would always follow me everywhere I went.

By early September I would have apples to give as a treat. Thunder, our brown quarter horse, would rub his muzzle against my cheek and neigh softly when he knew I had an apple to give him.

Late September Mama told me that it was almost time to go back to school. She had been working on a new school dress for me all summer. It was a beautiful blue gathered dress with ruffled sleeves and border lace.

The dress was ready; and so was I.

I enjoyed going to school. My Mother encouraged me to go, as she felt it was important to learn to read and write. She was schooled at home by her Mother, so when the new school house was built over by Wolf Pen Creek, she sent me there right away. That was in 1857. It was now 1859 and my little brother was starting school. He did not want to go.

Andrew cried on the first day of school as Mother got him ready. I had on my new dress and blue ribbons in my hair, ready to go. Mother marched Andrew over by my side and she demanded that I hold his hand. She handed me our lunch which was in a knapsack.

I could hear the school bell ringing from the schoolhouse bell tower as we went out the front door. The summons was being sounded out that school would be starting at nine o'clock sharp.

The shortest route to the school house was a rugged wagon road that cut through some fields and woods. The road ended at a narrow path, which we took to the Wolf Pen Creek Road. The one room school house was a short way up the road.

As Andrew and I arrived we saw other children walking across the front yard into the wide open front door. Miss Greenly stepped outside and waved at us, greeting every child with a smile. I was very happy to see Miss Greenly. She was my favorite teacher.

Andrew and I climbed up the wide steps and crossed the narrow porch and entered the school. We came into a small entryway that had two closets on either side, and the long rope which hung from the bell tower up on the roof. We entered the long classroom and Andrew stopped to look around. There were four rows of student desks, ten in each row. Towards the front were two rows of benches. That's where the youngest children sat. Miss Greenly's desk was just beyond the benches, and behind her desk, on the back wall, was a wide blackboard.

High windows were on both walls to our left and right. A wood stove sat snugly in the center aisle, unlit of course. It was too warm on the last day of September to fire it up.

Miss Greenly gathered the first-year students up front. She saw my brother holding onto my hand. He was trembling and looked terrified. She walked up to us and smiled.

"Ginny. I am glad to see you back for the start of the new school session. Is this your brother?"

"Yes." I replied. "This is Andrew."

"Andrew! I like that name. How old are you, Andrew?"

Miss Greenly placed her hand on Andrew's shoulders. "Well, you need to come and join our first-year students. I will show you, Andrew. Follow me."

Andrew went with Miss Greenly to the front and joined the other students his age. I went to my desk near the wood stove and sat down.

The day's lessons for each level were written on the board. There were several math problems written in chalk for the upper level students. Multiplication and division. I started working the problems on my slate board. Miss Greenly's helper, an older boy, checked our answers and recorded our progress in the teacher's grade book. I had them all correct. I knew that Miss Greenly would call me up front to work some of the problems after she finished teaching the younger children.

I sat next to Pelina, my best friend, and we often compared answers. A skinny girl with straight light brown hair, she was very precocious and at times down right daring. Last year she got me in trouble by insisting we take a short cut across the creek. We both ended up covered in mud and my mother was furious when I got home.

Miss Greenly was reading a story to the younger children. I glanced up to see how Andrew was doing. He seemed to be feeling better about school now. An eighth-grade girl took over instruction of the primers while Miss Greenly started teaching the upper graders.

She called the middle grade students one at a time to go up to the black board to solve the math problems. Then she put some fractions on the board and I was the first to be called up to give oral responses as she tapped each fraction with her long pointer stick. I had to quickly reduce each fraction to lowest terms in the mental exercise. I made some miscalculations and I turned red in the face. Miss Greenly tapped the fraction as I hesitated; it seemed like my mind just went blank as I started to panic. I was excused to sit down. I was not ready for drills on fractions on the first day! What made it worse was when Jimmy Skinner covered his mouth with his hand and let out a low laugh. Emma Taylor suppressed laughter, shook her head and stuck out her tongue at me.

Miss Greenly called Jimmy to go to the board next. He made many of the same mistakes that I had made. Miss Greenly shook her head and said that we were "rusty" after the long summer break, so we practiced reducing fractions until lunch time.

Andrew and I ate our lunch in the play yard in the shade of an old oak. Mother had packed us some rolls and cheese slices and juicy apples.

After lunch we practiced penmanship and then we read from our McGuffey Readers. At times, when I finished the story, my imagination allowed me to pull Emma Taylor's blonde hair and kick Jimmy Skinner in the seat of his pants.

Pelina could think of some prank to pull on them later.

It was a good school year. My reading and writing had blossomed. Miss Greenly was a good teacher.

We learned in April 1860 that Miss Greenly was getting married. Women teachers were not allowed to be married. This would therefore be Miss Greenly's last year at our school. I was very upset when I found out. What would I do without Miss Greenly?

School was never the same again. We had Mr. Bowles in the next school term. He was a terrible teacher. He did not care about teaching, he was doing it until he got a better job as an accountant.

Mr. Bowles was also a mean teacher. He had a leather strap hanging on the wall next to his desk and he did not hesitate to use it. He kept the bigger boys in line with it, even some of the girls. He showed no favorites. After a hard thrashing from Mr. Bowles, it was difficult to sit down.

It was a warm day in August 1862, Father had gone to the fields to work, Mother was in the house cooking as usual. I was able to slip away without her noticing, out through the side yard. I climbed the fence rails and walked out into the pasture. I found one of my favorite spots where I sat down on the grass. I saw the horses grazing in the distance. A slight breeze blew in my face and gently brushed my hair across my cheeks. I saw clover! I began to pick the clover flowers and braided the stems together to form a ringlet. This took me a long time to get a strand long enough. When I had completed a long enough strand of woven clover, I tied it around my head, wearing the clover like a crown. Now I imagined that I was a queen living in a palace!

Then I wandered down to the banks of the creek, and I looked into the murky waters. I could see some tadpoles swimming around. There were hoof prints in the sandy loam. I picked up a long stick and poked it into the mud, then into the water, stirring it around. This made ripples in the water that sparkled in the bright sunshine.

Mother was calling my name. I ran to her and listened as she told me to clean the house. I dusted all the rooms. I went into the parlor and dusted all the furniture in there. The room had two English windows side by side that faced towards the front of the house. This gave my favorite room plenty of light. This was the only room where we had fine furniture, like an upholstered love seat and chair, and side tables made of exquisite wood. I did a thorough job with my dusting, as I knew that Mother would run her fingers over the smooth wood to check for any dust residue. I swept the floors many times over to make the place look tidy; we were having company tonight.

Mother made a fancy meal of savory beef roast with all the trimmings. Our guests arrived, some country gents and their ladies from the church. I helped mother serve the meal, then sat down to enjoy a rare feast.

There was much conversation, but what really caught my ear was the talk about war. I did not understand what was going on, but the talk began to get heated, something about the North and South not getting along. Now the Union was sending an army to Louisville. An army in Louisville. I could not believe this! All this talk frightened me. I wondered what was going to happen. I felt very uneasy as I cleared the table.

It was now late August and we had brought in most of the field crops. I was thinking about starting school in a few weeks and hoping that we would get a nicer school master.

I got out of bed and pulled on my green plaid dress and ran down into the kitchen to see what was for breakfast.

Papa brought in the milk container; he had been out in the barn milking cows this morning. Mama was cooking on the pot belly stove. We sat down to a breakfast of ham and eggs, biscuits and milk. The fresh milk tasted so rich and smooth. My little brother sat across the small kitchen table from me and stuck out his tongue. I made a funny face and he giggled.

The biscuits were best smothered in honey and butter. The butter was running out. Today I would be at the butter churn, making a new batch.

I helped Mama clear off the table, while little brother ran off somewhere to play, and Father went back out to the barnyard to work.

Now was the time to churn the butter. I sat at a wooden stool in the middle of the kitchen and churned the cream with the plunger. It took a long time before the cream began to thicken into the consistency of butter. Mama sat in her rocker next to the kitchen window. She was sewing a new quilt. She was humming an old folk song as she worked. I loved to listen to her hum, it was so lovely as the melody carried throughout the entire house.

A slight breeze came through the open window, moving the lace curtains just a little. I could smell something sweet on the morning breeze, like freshly cut pine wood. Papa was sawing some wood.

Suddenly we heard shouting coming from the barnyard. It sounded like Papa was angry at someone. Mama and I stepped over to the window to see what is happening. There were soldiers out back in the barnyard, about four of them, all dressed in dark blue uniforms. What were these soldiers doing here? What did they want from us simple country folk?

We saw Father walking out of the barn towards the soldiers holding a riffle. He shouted, "Get off my land, you won't have my horses!"

One of the soldiers shouted back, demanding to have our prized horses. Mama looked so frightened.

A soldier pulled his pistol from the holster. "Stay back, or I'll put you in the ground!" he yelled.

Father did not back down. He continued to walk towards the soldiers, riffle pointed directly at the man with the drawn pistol.

I began to tremble, and my heart raced.

The soldier fired his pistol and father fell backwards, blood gushing from his forehead. Mama screamed. She ran out the back door, across the back yard to a wood pile next to a shed. She grabbed an axe from the wood pile and charged at the soldiers, screaming hysterically; shouting, "Get out of here, you devils!"

I have never seen such rage on Mama's face. She ran towards the men with the axe upraised, ready to strike them down. The same soldier who shot Papa drew his long curved-edged sword above his head, then swung it in a wide arc. The sword struck Mama's neck, slicing right through every muscle and tendon. Her decapitated head fell one direction, and her limp body immediately dropped to the ground.

I watched all of this in horror from the kitchen window. I was stunned, frozen for a moment, not knowing what to do. I realized that these soldiers would probably come to kill me too if they saw me, so I ran into the front room and grabbed my little brother, then escaped out the front of the house, running as fast as I could towards the corn field. I never looked back.

"What can I do? Where do I go? Run! Run for your life! Run silent, run swift!" a voice inside me cried.

I ran until I was out of breath, until my lungs were bursting for air. I tripped and fell, tearing the hem of my dress. I lay in the dirt, face down, and tore at the loose soil with my hands, sobbing.

"Ginny, don't cry!" I looked up and saw my little brother next to me. I felt like I must be strong for him. I stopped crying and raised up, looking into his eyes. He didn't know.

I got up and reached my hand out to him. "Come, we must get help!"

"What happened, Ginny? Where's Mama and Papa?" Andrew asked.

"We must get help!" I repeated.

We continued to walk through the corn to our neighbor's farm. I saw Ma Brown near her house washing clothes. We ran to her.

"Ma Brown! Ma Brown! Please help us! Please!"

"What's wrong, child?"

"Mama and Papa are hurt bad. Soldiers came and took our horses and...." My voice trailed off and I began to cry.

Ma Brown dropped what she was doing, told me and my brother to stay at her house, then she ran to get help. She ran to the grist mill and got several men to go with her. They found my Mama and Papa where they had been slain. Their bodies were placed in pine coffins and taken to the church cemetery. There was a funeral the next day and the pastor said some kind words, and everyone prayed at the grave site.

I noticed that there were mostly women at the funeral. Most of the men folk had left to fight in the Civil War, including my uncle Jed. He had joined the Union and was somewhere in Maryland. My Uncle Will, my Father's youngest brother, joined the Confederacy.

My little brother and I stayed with Ma Brown for a while, but she could not care for us. There was nobody working the farm; her husband and sons were fighting in the war. Arrangements were made for us to go to an orphanage in Louisville. I went back home to gather what I could... clothing, keepsakes and the like. Then I went and rounded up the farm animals that remained after the soldiers stole our horses.

I led them into the city of Louisville; all the animals followed me up East Main Street, past a large church with arches above the doors.

The goats were directly behind me, followed by sheep and cows. We were a sight, and I got many stares. As I neared downtown, I traversed several alleys in order to avoid the stares; Billy Goat Strut and Nanny Goat Strut. These alleys helped me to keep the animals in a line as we made our way through the city.

It was a cool fall morning, and I dressed in a crinmantle cape and a little pork pie hat.

Into Louisville I walked, a simple country girl all alone. Ladies and gents stared as I entered the city and paraded on by with a blank expression on my face. I was strong for the moment…yet a tear streamed down my cheek. It was very unusual to see a little girl bringing farm animals to the city markets; and the people looked and wondered about me and a long troupe of goats, sheep, cows and chickens. Through those narrow corridors I passed…cobblestone underfoot and rough masonry buildings on each side. Men looked up from their work at the livery and stared as I went, on towards the Bourbon Stock Yards. No more Mama and Papa, no more farm, no more horses, no more farm animals. Onwards to the stock yards.

I sold the last of our farm animals at the stock yards. With bitterness I took the money, money needed to survive. Still, I felt like I had betrayed my best friends.

I went back and got my little brother. We dressed in our finest clothing. I wore my yellow silky dress and a white bonnet.

We departed for the orphanage. I held my little brother's hand as we walked along Market Street in Louisville. Squared paving stones were underfoot. I looked up and saw an imposing red brick building; it looked austere. It was St. Vincent's Orphanage. I remembered the spires on the building looked much like an Old-World fortress. We went through the gate to our new home.

I was admitted to St. Vincent's immediately. Andrew was taken to the boy's orphanage, St. Thomas in Bardstown. We entered the orphanages in the fall of 1862 and remained there for a very long time.

In the early years at St. Vincent, I went into a long period of depression. This was a very bad time in my life.

One day I was laying on a blanket that was spread out on the front lawn of the orphanage. I was in a dress, laying in a fetal position face down, with my legs drawn up under my belly. I would stay in this position for a long time, and I felt that nobody cared about me. I did not talk to anyone. I had become mute. I remember that there were some women standing in the walkway wearing wide long gathered dresses that went all the way to the ground. One lady was talking to a well-dressed man in a suede suit.

I don't know what they were discussing. I just remember feeling so sad, lost, and alone. I could hear them discussing something; perhaps they were talking about me. But I did not want to talk to anyone, I just wanted everyone to leave me alone. I withdrew into a world of silence, I hung my head, and did not respond when I was addressed by adults.

It may be that I was not neglected, but instead chose this posture of resistance. I became uncooperative, at times unruly. So perhaps the well-dressed man and spiffy women were there to help me come out of my isolation, to do some novel 19th century psychology on me. I am sure that their intentions were good, trying to help a disturbed orphan girl. Anyway, I don't think that whatever they did worked, I remained in my solitude for quite some time.

Then I became very sick with the measles. I had a high fever and my face had bumps and sores. A kind nurse took care of me and she brought my fever down by keeping me hydrated with wet towels and some medicine. She saved my life. I came very close to death. At times, I might have felt like dying, but something inside me struggled for life. I did not want to die like that.

There were some good, caring people on the staff, but they could never take the place of my parents; the warmth, love and nurture that I had received when I was with them. I missed my parents and the farm. Now everything was gone. My life had been shattered by the mean evil soldiers, they were murderers. I wanted them to hang for what they did.

I could not see my little brother. I lost contact with him for many years.

Once I recovered from the measles I started to come out of my deep depression. I made friends with the other girls in my ward. I was especially close with Katherine and Lillian. We read books together and went for long walks with the sisters into the city. One of the younger sisters, Sister Abigale, took us under her wing. She walked us to the city park to play games like croquet and badminton. The activities helped me to regain my ambition.

We attended the orphanage school run by the sisters Mondays through Fridays. My academics improved under the demanding instruction. On Saturdays we had religious studies, and of course church on Sunday.

The fact that there was a war going on meant that there were few adoptions. Most families were challenged to the limit and were on a day to day survival for existence. Men had gone to serve in the war, draining many homes of resources.

The orphanage did serve as a shelter for us girls from the stark realities of that war. We were treated well and had all our daily provisions on a timely basis, and good meals prepared in the kitchen. The sisters taught us the value of hard work.

Katherine, Lillian and I were assigned to work details in the kitchen. We were on duty early in the morning, having our breakfast late just before classes started at 9 AM. We also worked the supper detail from 4:30 to 6 PM.

We would be at the kitchen at 6 AM making biscuits. Sisters Mary and Patricia would be frying sausage, bacon and eggs. Sometimes we made fried potatoes and johnnycakes.

Johnnycakes were also popular for supper. We prepared a lot of pork and sausage, roasted beef and potatoes, fruit and vegetables when in season. After we made the johnnycakes, Katherine, Lillie and I would help serve the girls in the dining hall. The sisters were very strict on how much we served portions. One slice of meat, one scoop of mashed potatoes with a dab of gravy, one johnnycake, and a fruit or vegetable. With three meals a day we ate better than many folks in those times.

I remember that once there was a shortage of food in the fall of 1863. We did not know what happened to our food shipment over a two-week period. Apparently, our supply wagons had been intercepted by some Union soldiers and they took our food. We had to eat a lot of johnnycakes and beans for a while.

The thought of these Union soldiers plundering our food made me furious. It made me think of the evil soldiers who had killed my Ma and Pa and stole our horses. I had come to hate all Union soldiers.

I was not the only one. Many people in the city of Louisville had come to resent the presence of what was seen as an occupation army. It was not at all uncommon to hear the slogan "Yankee go home!" being shouted in the streets. People were weary of the drunken soldiers staggering through the streets at all hours of the day and night, the gambling and constant brawls.

By May of 1864 most of the Union troops were leaving Louisville, headed to Chattanooga to join forces marching toward Atlanta. Those rampaging soldiers went to Atlanta and burned it to the ground, looting and ravaging the Confederacy.

1865

One day in July 1865 Sister Reese came and said that I had some visitors. I went with Sister Reese to the orphanage lobby and I saw my brother Andrew there with a man that I did not recognize. Andrew had grown so much since I had last seen him. He was now twelve years old, three years younger than me.

We embraced, and I cried. I was so happy to see him.

The man smiled at me and introduced himself as Uncle Will. I had not seen him in many years. He had been a soldier and had been away for a very long time in Memphis. He was my father's youngest brother.

Sister Reese smiled at me. "Your Uncle Will has signed adoption papers for you, Ginny.

You have a new home now. Please do not forget us and come visit us once in a while."

I could not believe that I was leaving the orphanage. It was like taking my first baby steps. This had been my home for almost four years.

I packed all my belongings and said a tearful farewell to all my friends at the orphanage and to the sisters.

When I left the orphanage, the Civil War had ended, and President Lincoln was shot. It would take a long time for me to heal from the wounds inflicted by that war. This was true for the entire country.

Uncle Will

The war was over. Men were returning in droves. In Louisville, some men fought for the Confederacy, and others fought for the Union. This was true for my Uncle Jed and Uncle Will. They were on opposing sides. When the war was over, Uncle Jed returned to his farm. His wife died years ago, so he was alone.

There were a lot of tensions during this time. There were also hundreds of freed slaves in the city, suddenly without a place to live or work. It was into this time of uncertainty that I departed the orphanage to make a fresh start.

Andrew and I went with our Uncle Will. We lived with him and his new wife, Nellie Belle. He had taken over my Mama and Papa's land and had worked it back into a productive farm.

Pelina, my best friend from my school days, came to visit often. We rode horses together. Having Pelina close helped me to adjust to the challenges of returning to the farm. It was difficult with the bad memories of my parent's murder. Now, with Pelina's help, I was beginning to resemble my former self before the bad things happened in my life.

We loved to ride one of the dark brown steeds named Lightning. We rode that horse up and down a long green pasture. The farm had several wide expanses of pastureland surrounded by wooded areas. We rode together, me on the front and her holding on to my waist from the back. I was wearing a long maroon colored dress; Pelina also wore a long flowing dress fashionable for the time. We rode straddling the horse like a man. People would look surprised to see this and asked why we did not ride like proper ladies. No doubt it was more fun this way, and we wanted to ride Lightning fast. We would ride up and down the length of the pasture, laughing all the way, our long hair flowing in the wind. We loved the spirited horse, he made the ride all the more thrilling.

April 1867

I lived with my uncle until I was almost 17. My little brother grew up into a strong young man. Life was good once again, but I began to question my uncle about taking over the farm. Wasn't I the rightful heir? Was he going to take it away from me?

My uncle and his wife were good to my brother and me for a long period of time, but when I was about 17 things began to change for the worse. There was constant bickering, my uncle seemed to be having a hard time with the farm and with his marriage.

His wife was much younger, twenty-three; even so she manipulated him. She always seemed to want more and more. And the more that I learned about her past, the less I got along with her.

Then there was the issue of the farm. I felt like the farm should belong to me and my brother, that was what my parents would have wanted. But they were now the sole owners of the deed by rights of having worked the farm for 2 years. This led to many fights. I could not stand either of them anymore.

Then one-day Nellie Belle (my uncle's wife) tells me that she used to be a saloon girl in Memphis. She knows how to get her way with men, she tells me. "Honey, why don't ya' go to Louisville, you are a pretty girl, trim and fit. You can get yourself anything you want there. It's time you moved on, Ginny."

Her words stung like the bite of a black widow spider. I cried myself to sleep that night. I woke up before sunrise, laying there in bed, thinking about my life. I remembered all the good times I had at the farm when Mama and Papa were alive, and the wonderful times that I had with Pelina riding horses, laughing away all my cares. Now my house and land were stolen out from under me. I had to fight back.

Circumstances forced my decision. I left for Louisville the following week.

I had to get away from my uncle and his conniving wife. I decided to go out and start a new life on my own; to some degree this was testing my wings. I knew that I had to make it on my own. I could not depend on those who were taking away my rightful inheritance.

I told my brother of my plans, and at first, he tried to persuade me to stay, but in the end, he understood my actions. Pelina helped me to pack. She also supported my decision. I gave Lightening to her and he had a good home on her father's farm, where I was able to visit often and ride.

My bags were ready to go, and I rode into the city with Pelina and her mother in a carriage. They helped me to find a place to live.

I found a room at a widow's house. Louisville had many Civil War widows. It must have been so lonely for them, most having lost husbands and sons in the gruesome war. The house was a typical 19th century Victorian style residence south of Market.

I found work at a garment factory in the warehouse district. I worked with other young women at the factory, but there was not much time for socializing, as we had to keep a steady pace or face termination by a mean, burly male supervisor who smelled of liquor. I hated the job and yearned for better times. The factory was dirty with deplorable conditions, and I had to put in 12 hours a day, sunrise to sunset. By the time I got home to my rented room I was drained.

One evening on the way home from work our horse-drawn street car passed some taverns and card rooms near Fourth Street and Main.

Brilliantly lit up with gas lights, these places seemed inviting compared to my horrid existence at the factory. I was curious; this nightlife seemed the attraction, a nice escape from the drudgery of the garment factory.

The following weekend, I went out with some of the girls from work and my best friends, Pelina and Katherine. We all wanted to experience the nightlife firsthand. I was able to get the weekend off from the factory, and my plans were laid for a weekend of fun and adventure. I invited my two friends to come stay with me. When I got home from work, Pelina was waiting for me on the front steps of the house. I took her up to the second floor and showed her my room. We had many stories to tell and much gossip to catch up on.

Katherine arrived along with my friends from work, Sarah and Victoria. It was time to get ready for our evening out on the town. We put on our layered bustle dresses, fixed one another's hair and applied make-up, perfumes and jewelry. I must say we all looked very elegant in our lovely attire. Of course, bonnets were not worn with our evening dresses. Katherine's long red hair was much too beautiful to hide.

We walked to the street corner to wait for the horse-drawn street car. Soon we boarded the car and were on our way. The coach entered Fourth Street, close to the central business district. Passing several stores and banks, we disembarked near some hotels. Not far from the hotels were several taverns. There was music in the air and laughter spilled from the many establishments on either side of the street.

We were attracted to one of the larger taverns that was very busy with customers, and we could hear a fiddle and banjo playing some lively tunes. The door stood open, and inside we could see many crowded rooms. The bar area was in the front, and in a side room there was music and many people dancing. Another area to the left was a card room with several tables, where gamblers sat holding their playing cards.

We stood at the door looking inside for a long time, trying to get our confidence up to go inside. I kept thinking about all the sermons I'd listened to when I was young, about the sins of dancing and liquor, and how women who do such things are vixens. I think my friends were having the same dreadful thoughts.

Some very rowdy people got off one of the coaches in the street and pressed their way towards the saloon. One of the women in the group smiled at us.

"Come on! Come on!" She told us, motioning for us to enter. We walked into the bar shaking from head to toe.

Here we stood in a tavern of all places, four young ladies from an astute upbringing, well versed in the ways of proper Christian conduct. I kept thinking, "my, what would the man of the cloth say now?" I felt uncomfortable, it was too warm in there, with the smell of smoke and liquor everywhere. I was about ready to turn around and walk out, but the music and dancing from the adjoining room was riveting. The dancing was so energetic, the ladies' dresses spinning around, high kicks, partners moving in circles arm in arm.

We edged closer to the dance floor. Pelina knew many of the dance moves, and she showed us the ropes. This was just in the nick of time. The men were eyeing us from the moment we entered the bar, and soon we were all out on the dance floor, swinging and spinning to the rhythm of the music.

I must have danced with three different men before I met Walter. Walter was attractive, twenty-three years old, and very muscular. About five feet ten, he had light sandy wavy hair and gray eyes. We danced through the rest of the night, and he was a natural at it. I learned rapidly with his lead. I had never had so much fun in all my life. He bought me some drinks, gin (gin for Ginny) mixed for a lady's taste. Everything felt just fine now, I was hot and sweaty, but so was everyone else out on the dance floor. It was an evening that none of us would ever soon forget.... I danced until my feet felt numb.

Walter and I rested at a table in the bar area. Pelina and my other friends joined us, so we put some tables together. We had another round of drinks. There were many men sitting and standing around our table; we had caused quite a stir. I gave all my attention to Walter.

Walter told me that he worked on the riverboats, that he had started out as a deck hand, but now he was a pilot.

I told him about my life. He listened with keen interest, shaking his head in dismay when I described how my parents had been brutally murdered by the soldiers.

"Union soldiers did this?" He asked.

"Yes" I said. "They wore dark blue uniforms. They were Union soldiers."

When I told him how my uncle had stolen my farm, his eyes flashed with anger.

"Someday we will have to get your farm back," he said.

I wondered if he were serious.

I wrote down my address on a slip of paper. I was anxious to see him again.

We stayed until the bar closed at half past midnight. There were no coaches at this hour, so Walter and another man that Pelina had met at the bar walked us home. We held hands as we walked up Fifth Street.

Walter and I embraced when we got to the door of my rooming house. We set a date for the following Saturday for diner; I could not wait.

Pelina left the next day. I lay in bed thinking about Walter with my eyes closed. I imagined him pulling me close, whispering words of love in my ear. His lips came close to mine, we kissed.

I woke up with the sun streaming through the window. Time for work. I hated having to go to that horrible factory job, the mean male supervisor yelling at poor girls until they cried. He seemed to especially enjoy humiliating the female workers. Some girls were physically abused.

Around mid-week he came into the work room and began yelling at me, spewing all sorts of insults. He was so close that I could smell the liquor on his breath. He claimed that my work was not acceptable. He yanked me from my seat by the hair, and he was about to lay his hands on me. I kicked him so hard below the belt that he immediately fell to the floor grimacing in pain. "You wicked winch!" he yelled. All the other workers clapped and cheered. I became an instant hero there.

I was fired immediately. I went home and cried in my bed. I began to hate this city life, I yearned to be back on the farm. I missed my parents.

Without work what little money I had would run out fast. I did not make very much money at the factory. I barely had enough to buy food once my room rent was paid. By Saturday I was eating the last of the crumbs from my bread drawer.

On Saturday morning, I received a message from Walter stating that we were going to dine in a fancy restaurant. Formal dress would be required. I took the nicest clothing from my closet, a velvet maroon layered bustle dress.

Walter arrived at seven o'clock with flowers in hand. He wore a vested suit and bow tie. We went to town in style in a luxury carriage that had an upholstered interior. I felt like the queen!

There were many fine restaurants in downtown Louisville in 1867. Walter took me to the most expensive one. Fine woodwork, plush carpets, chandeliers; the place was stunning.

We ordered the house specialty; roasted pheasant. We also had some of the house wine.

I think that I drank a little too much wine. By the time we arrived at my rooming house in the plush carriage, I was in a very giddy mood. Walter carried me up the stairs and sat me down on a couch that was in the second-floor foyer.

He sat next to me and told me funny stories from his riverboat adventures. We laughed, then he leaned over and kissed me on the lips passionately. He suddenly sprang to his feet and stripped down to his waist! I could see tattoos on his muscular arms, chest and back, mostly tattoos of birds with outstretched wings. He knelt in front of me, slowly lifting up my dress above my knees.

There was a sudden noise. A door swung open on the other side of the foyer, and there stood my landlady, Mrs. Peacher. She looked extremely angry. "What do you think yore' doing there, young man? I'll have none of this in my house!"

I quickly lowered my dress. My face was now crimson red.

"Get yore' clothes on, boy! This is a God fearin' house and this kind of conduct will not be tolerated here!"

Walter dressed hurriedly, looking anxious to get away from the old bitty. She continued to give us the tongue lashing.

"I am just appalled, especially at you, Ginny. I thought that you were a fine upstanding young lady with virtue. Was I ever wrong about that! I want you out of my house! You get out by tomorrow morning!"

"No, no, Mrs. Peacher!" I pleaded, then started to cry. "I have no place to go!"

Walter came over and held my hands firmly.

"Ginny", he said calmly. "It's okay. I will find a place for you to stay. I will take care of you now."

Walter came through with his promise. The next day I was living in one of Louisville's finest hotels near Main Street. Walter paid all my room and board.

The Hotel

I had fallen in love with Walter. However, I was not too secure with the arrangements we had. Don't get me wrong, it was wonderful to be his "one and only true love", as he called me. He treated me like a lady, gave me exquisite gold and diamond jewelry, wined and dined me out on the town, and we made love. But he would not marry me; at least not yet. He was a riverman, and his duties kept him away for long periods of time, so he was not ready for a long-term commitment.

I was now living the life of luxury in a downtown Louisville hotel. The hotel was very nice, wedged between other commercial buildings near Main Street. The front lobby was elegantly furnished, with a long clerk's desk on the left side when you entered from the street. Mr. Weaver, the desk clerk, would always look up and smile at me when I walked by. "Well, hello, Miss Ginny!" He would say, peering at me through his wire rimmed glasses. I would smile at him and walk to the balustraded stairs, holding up the hem of my long dress as I climbed several steps to the second floor. From the stairs, I entered a large foyer area, complete with couches and reading chairs, side tables, and a big fireplace. There were ornate brass gas lamps mounted along the walls, always lit at night.

Two hallways opened from the left and right side of the foyer. My room was the second door down the corridor to the right. The room faced the street.

I had a good-sized room with two queen sized poster beds, desk, chairs, and a table. On a countertop, next to a large mirror, there was a large matching ceramic pitcher and sink. There was also a small ice box where I could store meat and milk. Two windows faced street side, and I usually opened the long drapes so that I could view the activity on the street.

Walter would be away for extended periods of time working on the riverboats. I missed him dearly when he was gone, every time he left on that huge behemoth steamboat, belching its black smoke from two tall stacks, tears would fill my eyes.

Oftentimes when Walter was away, my friends would stay with me. Pelina came and Sara, one of the girls from the garment factory, and Katherine. Sometimes we would stand in front of the hotel on the sidewalk in our fine Victorian dresses. We'd chat, giggle, and sometimes go for a stroll through the city, shopping in the many fine specialty shops downtown.

When Sara and Pelina left, I usually stayed in my room, leaving only for my evening meal at the restaurant. I occasionally ate meals in my room.

When I was alone I would write in my journal. It had a tanned leather cover, and inside the front cover, I had written my name in scrawled cursive letters in blue ink from a fountain pen. I had recorded all of the important events of my life therein, from my earliest memories. Now I was writing down my most personal thoughts, my dreams of a happy life with Walter. He would marry me someday and never be away from me again.

Sometimes I got lost in my thoughts, sitting at the desk in my room writing in my journal. The pen and paper were my constant companions, to write was a release from my solitude.

June 25, 1867

I met a lady last night at dinner. I told her about Walter, all about his position on the steam boat, and how he was providing for me. Then she said something that puzzled me. She said that she wondered if he (Walter) was doing "something else". Indeed, she questioned if he were making a sufficient income on a riverboat to support me and to give me the lavish gifts that he showered on me when he returned from his long excursions.

What did she mean by "something else?" What else could he be doing? I should have prodded her to tell me more of her suspicions, but I really did not give her comments much consideration at the time, she was probably just envious of me.

July 5, 1867 Stage Coach Driver

I was still sitting at the desk in my hotel room, with my journal in front of me, thinking about the woman I had met at dinner

She was probably simply jealous of my expensive jewelry, and for her to put such thoughts in my head was certainly unkind. But then again, I did not know everything when it came to riverboats. I had never been on one yet, although I wanted to join Walter sometime on his boat. What other things could Walter be doing on board? Was he hiding something from me?

My thoughts were suddenly interrupted by some loud commotion out on the street. The windows were open, and I could hear what sounded like a mad man shouting below. I walked over to the window. I was shocked at what I saw.

A stagecoach driver was beating his horses with a whip! I was so angry that I ran from my room and down the stairs so fast that I tore the hem of my dress. I ran out into the street just as the coach driver was on the back lash. I grabbed the end of the whip and wrapped it around a hitching post. As he drew his arm forwards, the whip handle fell from his hand. He turned around and glared at me, his face contorted with rage.

"What cha' hell ya' doin'!" He shouted.

I pulled on the whip strap until the handle was in my hand.

"Gimme back my whip ya' stupid girl! I've a mind to use it on ya'!"

"How dare you beat these horses!" I yelled in a fury. "How about if I use the whip on you!"

"Ya' wouldn't dare!"

I glared at him, and for a moment I saw in his face the evil soldier who killed my parents.

I swung the whip in a wide arc in front of me. The coach driver backed up as I approached him swinging the whip.

"Whoa, girl, what cha' matter with ya'?"

A crowd began to gather around the stagecoach. Everyone began to cheer me on. I guess they also had enough of the mean driver. I struck the whip across his arms as he tried to cover his face. He winced in pain as a long red streak appeared on his flesh. Some of the onlookers began to laugh. Apparently, this was providing their entertainment for the afternoon. But I was dead serious as I raised the whip to strike him again. This time I knocked off his hat.

"What the hell!" He yelped.

Someone grabbed me by the wrist and stopped my next swing.

"Stop! Now!" It was a police officer. "Put down the whip!" he demanded.

I handed the whip to him.

"Lock her up, officer!" The driver said, holding on to his arm in pain. "She be a crazed girl, the likes of her needs to be put away!"

"You were beating these poor horses to death. You're the one that needs to be locked up!" I shot back with fire. "These horses look like the ones that my father bred before he was murdered by those thieves. Yes, they look just like them! If he were here would have taken you out!"

There was a murmur in the crowd. I heard a man talking close by: "Say, isn't she that Chamberlain girl? Why, I knew her father, had a horse ranch out near Harrods Creek."

The man looked at me. "Ginny? Are you Ginny?"

I returned his gaze. "Yes." I replied. "I am Ginny Chamberlain."

July 6, 1867

The next day was Saturday, and I was on my way to buy fresh vegetables at the Market Street stand when I saw the stage coach driver again. He was walking down Main with four Union soldiers. They stopped and chatted in front of the Garmin Hotel. I stopped and stared at them, hiding behind my pink parasol.

They were talking loudly as though they were in an argument. Then there were loud bursts of laughter. These soldiers seemed familiar to me. I was sure that they were the same men who had killed my parents. I would never forget the faces of those men. The memory was etched in my mind forever. Were these the same men? I had to make sure. I had to learn more about them and how they knew the stage coach driver.

They walked into the hotel. I followed them at a distance. From the lobby I saw them going up to the second landing on the stairs. I kept my eye on them. They talked loudly the whole time, so it was easy to keep track of their movements. Not only did they talk loudly, they stomped their feet wherever they went. Once up on the second floor, I saw them walking down a corridor to their room. They went inside and slammed the door. I quickly walked up the corridor and read the room number on the door. Room 24.

I stood at the door for a long time, listening to their conversation. I heard a lot of bragging about looting southern plantation houses in Georgia. Then there was some heated discussion on how to split the spoils.

I felt sick to my stomach knowing that these corrupt men had plundered in the war and committed all sorts of atrocities.

One of the men said, "Hey, Sarge, how did you get that red mark on your arm?"

I heard more laughter. Sarge answered "Some crazed girl got ahold of my horse whip and hit me with it the other day when I was keepin' my horses in line. I still got a festering sore here that won't go away, and it's been a hurtin' real bad."

"You were knocked around by some girl out on the street?"

All the men roared in laughter again.

So, sarge was the stage coach driver. I felt a sense of satisfaction in learning that the whip mark that I had inflicted on his arm was now a festering sore.

"Did you know this girl, sarge?" Another man asked. There was more hysterical laughter.

"No, but they said that her name is Ginny Chamberlain, and her father owned a horse ranch near here."

There was a long pause in the conversation. I was shocked to learn that this "sarge" knew my name. I remembered from the stagecoach incident that one of the men bystanders said my name and recognized me from my father's farm.

"If memory serves me right," another man said, "that was the Chamberlain farm where we stole those horses at the beginning of the war, wasn't it Flynt?"

"Yeah, after sarge killed the man and his wife we ransacked the house. Chamberlain was the name on the documents we found in a desk drawer."

I was not sure who Flynt was, but now I knew for sure that these were the same men who had killed my parents.

I was feeling weak and my knees were shaking. I ran back to the stairs and quickly went down to the hotel lobby. I stepped into the ladies' powder room and splashed some water on my face. I looked in the mirror. My face was red, and tears streamed down my cheeks. Suddenly everything was spinning around. I held onto the side of the countertop. I almost fainted. I took some deep breaths in order to regain my composure.

I ran out of the hotel and walked briskly to the central police station. It was very busy and crowded there. I sat on a bench for a long time waiting to talk to a sergeant Bowers.

It was almost one o'clock when the police sergeant finally called me into his cluttered office. I sat on a chair in front of his small desk. He placed a blank police report form on the desk and looked at me.

"Please state your name for the record."

"Ginny Chamberlain."

The sergeant wrote my name at the top of the report. He cleared his throat.

"Okay, Ginny, you are reporting a crime?"

"Yes."

"And what is the nature of this crime?"

"My parents were murdered. The men who murdered them are staying at the Garmin Hotel in room 24."

The sergeant had a puzzled look.

"Why do you suspect these men of the murder of your parents? What evidence do you have to support such a claim?"

"I overheard them talking, and they said that they did it."

"And when and where did this murder happen?"

"Five years ago, on our farm near Harrods Creek. Soldiers came and murdered my Pa and Ma. Then they stole our horses and were never caught."

The sergeant raised his eyebrows and put down his pen.

"Well, first of all, this happened out of our jurisdiction. That far out of the city would fall under the Jefferson County Sheriff's office. But let me just say that you are going to have difficulty getting an investigation going from any law enforcement agency. Six years ago, all of our area was under martial law, hence local law enforcement became a side show."

"But these murderers are here in Louisville, and I know where they are staying! I heard them talking in their room about my parent's murder! They said that they did it! Why can't you arrest them?"

"Ginny, we have no evidence that they committed any crime. Do you have any witnesses or sworn testimony?"

"I was the only witness!" I cried.

The sergeant leaned forward in his chair and examined my face.

"Ginny, I have a deputy here on duty who's told me that you were attacking a stage coach driver with a horse whip the other day. This certainly does raise suspicion about your intentions here, if not to your own sanity."

"What!" I shouted. "Are you saying that I am out of my mind? My parents were brutally murdered by these evil soldiers! How dare you question my sanity!"

The police sergeant fidgeted in his chair and appeared to be uncomfortable. He heaved a long deep sigh.

"Well, Ginny. Since soldiers were involved, it is a military affair at this point, and it always was. You need to take this to the provost officer at Newport."

I knew then and there that I would get no help from law enforcement. It was useless to expect any justice against the soldiers who murdered my parents. I got up and was ready to leave.

"Wait a minute," the sergeant said. "Tell me again the hotel and room where these men are staying."

"They are at the Garmin Hotel in room 24."

He wrote down the information. Then he looked up at me with a weak smile.

"I will tell my deputies to keep an eye on these characters. They seem like a bunch of troublemakers. Thank you for the information."

After Sergeant Bowers said that, I felt a little better as I left the police headquarters and walked slowly back to my hotel room.

I could see the Garmin Hotel from my second-floor window. It was a small hotel on the opposite side of the street. Not directly across, but towards the left as I peered out my window.

I was prepared to leave on a moment's notice if the men emerged from the hotel. I planned to watch them like a hawk and follow their movements everywhere they went.

Katherine lived in a boarding house not far from my hotel. I sent a messenger there with a note explaining my situation and asking for her help. We had remained close friends since our orphanage days. I knew that I could count on her.

She arrived about an hour later with a large handbag stuffed with provisions. She wore a simple cotton summer dress. I was happy and relieved to see her. I needed someone that could give me support and confidence. Katherine was the type of person that I could always count on in times of need. I told her about the soldiers and my intentions concerning them.

I pushed a table and chairs over by the window so that we could sit down and watch the hotel down the street.

We dined on some chicken that I had in my ice box, with some cold tea. We talked about our days at the orphanage. The time passed quickly. Now it was beginning to get dark outside.

There was a knock at the door. I opened it. Pelina stood there wearing a beautiful pink calico dress.

So much had happened that I had completely forgotten that we had planned a girl's night out this evening.

"Pelina! I forgot that this is Saturday night!"

I told her about the events of the day. She was very understanding and very willing to offer her assistance in tracking the soldiers.

I set out a bowl of fruit and lemonade. We chatted and joked around for quite some time, when Katherine suddenly pointed out the window and shouted, "I think that's them!"

The sarge and the soldiers had just left the hotel and they walked towards Fourth Street on the wide sidewalk.

"Yes! That's them!" I exclaimed. "Let's go and follow behind and see where they are going!"

We walked briskly to the stairs and descended to the hotel lobby. We made our way past the clerk's desk and exited the building. Looking up the street we saw sarge and his soldier friends walking slowly down the sidewalk. They were undoubtedly headed for the taverns and card rooms along Fourth Street and Main.

By now it was completely dark. The lamplighter was coming up the wide street, lighting the gas street lights with his long pole. The city became very lively as the gas lamps lit up the night. Taverns and card rooms were filling up fast with patrons.

We stopped at the corner of Fourth and Main and watched as the sarge and his buddies went into one of the larger taverns with one of the most notorious card rooms in Louisville. We crossed the street and stood in front of the tavern, trying to muster enough courage to enter. It was crowded out front, and even more so within the establishment. The sounds of music and laughter became louder every time someone opened the door.

We slowly inched our way into the tavern. The sarge and his men were at one of the tables in the card room. I started to panic. If the sarge saw us he would recognize me immediately from the stagecoach encounter a few days past.

We rushed into the ladies' powder room. I told Pelina and Katherine about my fear of being seen by the sarge. Pelina said that she could disguise me with makeup.

She pulled a small makeup case from her purse. Pelina layered dark red lipstick on my mouth and rouge on my cheeks. Then she applied white face powder and black liner to my lashes and brows. Next, she tied my hair back off my shoulders. I did not even recognize myself in the mirror when she was finished.

Pelina and Katherine also put on some makeup in moderation. They did not need a disguise. The thick layers of makeup caked on my face made me very uncomfortable.

Once we returned to the bar area we were swooped upon by scores of men asking us to dance. I refused as I wanted to keep an eye on sarge. Katherine and Pelina were soon out on the dance floor, dancing with several partners.

I was abashed when men came towards me offering money. I must have told a dozen or so men "no" before I realized what was happening. Some men started to laugh and shouted, "How much does this wench want?" Then another man yelled "She must be one of them high class saloon girls. Better win a few rounds of poker to get the likes of her!" There was more laughter. I was embarrassed and humiliated. I ran to the ladies' powder room and washed off all the makeup.

I stood there looking at myself in the mirror. My eyes were watering. I took some deep breaths, wishing that the night was over and done with. I had to face my fears and my enemy. They were out there gambling and drinking. I was consumed with a hatred for these wretched men. I knew that I needed to be strong.

I walked back out to the bar room floor. Pelina and Katherine were there looking for me. Katherine and Pelina were also having problems with advances from unscrupulous men. Wearing makeup in a tavern was not a good idea. You were seen as being a loose woman for doing so. A girl could not get much respect by visiting such establishments in the first place; and the makeup only made it worse.

We moved closer to the cloak room, away from the most annoying men. We couldn't see the card room very well from there, but we were able to see the sarge and his men in one of the bar room mirrors.

A table became available not far from where we were standing. We quickly went to the table and sat down. A waiter brought us some popcorn, peanuts, and pretzels, saying that it was on the house.

I sat facing away from the card room so the sarge couldn't see me We ordered some hard cider to wash down the tid-bits.

I started to feel better. It seemed more like a girl's night out on the town. We were having a good time, laughing and making good conversation. The tavern was becoming more crowded and noisy as the night wore on, and the piano, fiddles and banjos sounded out the music endlessly as partners danced to the rhythm.

We noticed that sarge and his buddies were playing poker with many of the tavern patrons, and after cleaning them out, they challenged others to join in the game. They cleaned out more than a dozen men. It was obvious that they had a free dealing racket going on, and they were raking in the money fast.

There was a loud argument. I turned around to watch as several men were yelling at sarge and his friends. Their free wheeling and dealing tactics had been exposed. I heard accusations leveled of "stacked deck!"

Sarge and his buddies were seasoned fighters. Soon several men were laying on the floor in pools of blood.

They bullied their way out of the card room, walking toward our table. I tried to cover my face quickly with a Chinese hand fan, but it was too late. Sarge saw me.

Sarge stopped in his tracks and pointed at me. "It's her!" He shouted. "There she is, boys! That's Ginny Chamberlain!"

Sarge lunged towards me, knocking over several chairs. He grabbed me by the hair. "I'll show you, you little vixen! Look at my arm! See what you did with the horse whip? You're going to get it now!"

"Leave me alone!" I cried.

Katherine threw the pitcher of cider in his face. Pelina hit him on the head with a chair. Several men came to help us, and there were punches thrown as a great melee broke out.

I ran from the tavern, followed by Katherine and Pelina.

"They're getting away!" I heard Sarge shout as we ran to the street.

"Let's get out of here!" I screamed. "Run!"

We ran down the street, weaving around several carriages. Sarge and the soldiers chased us towards Market Street. The street was well lit on both sides and was busy with bargain seekers waiting for the produce stands to close and barter off their remaining food stock. When we got to Floyd Street we stopped, out of breath. We looked up Market towards Third. Sarge and the soldiers were in hot pursuit.

We ran up Floyd Street and turned down an alley. It was very dark there with plenty of places to hide on either side.

It was very difficult to see anything in the alley. We stopped behind a market where there were high stacks of burlap bags and barrels lined up in several rows. A few cats went scurrying as we wedged ourselves within the stock piles. There was a gap between the barrels where we could peer through. We saw sarge and his men stop at the head of the alley. A gas street lamp lit the area where they were standing. We got a good look at their faces.

"Where did they go?" Sarge yelled in an angry voice.

"They could have gone up that alley," bellowed one of the men.

"Alright, Josh. You and Flynt check the alley. Me and Gus will go around the block and meet you at the other end."

Flynt and the other soldier started to move slowly up the alley. Flynt held a bowie knife.

Sarge turned and glanced up the alley at them. "If you find those girls I want them in one piece. We can always have a little fun now, boys! The night's still young!"

The men laughed and hooted loudly as they split up to widen their search.

We cowered in dread behind the barrels. If we were caught we knew what these evil men were capable of doing, they were war criminals and they would not hesitate to inflict indescribable indignities on us and then slit our throats.

The men started to search the stock piles. They pushed a stack of barrels over, making a loud crash. We were ready to run when a shop door opened, and a burly looking man stepped into the alley holding a shot gun.

"Who's there?" He shouted. He saw the two soldiers holding the knife next to the fallen barrels.

"Get outta' here or I'll blow your brains out!" He yelled. He aimed the gun and fired a warning shot down low. Both men ran back to the street, one of them limping; apparently, he was grazed in the foot, and he was crying out in agony.

"Let's make a run for it!" Pelina exclaimed, motioning for us to follow. We ran to the next cross street. Sarge and Gus were waiting there for us. He pulled his knife out quickly and pointed it at my chest, then let out a disgusting laugh. Katherine jumped on his back and got a choke hold on him. Gus stood there in a daze, undoubtedly intoxicated. Pelina and I grabbed sarge's arm and pushed the knife away from me. The three of us were overpowering him.

"Gus! Help me!" He cried.

Gus tried to get Katherine off his back, but he couldn't. I jabbed my nails deep into the festering sore on the sarge's arm. He screamed in agony. The whole time Katherine was beating him in the head. Somehow, his holster belt became unfastened and it fell to the sidewalk. I quickly reached down and grabbed the belt and drew the gun from the holster.

When sarge and Gus saw me holding the gun, they immediately ran up the dark alley. I pulled the trigger back and fired two shots as they fled. Thankfully, Walter had showed me how to fire a gun.

I was not very good at firing, and I was shaking when I shot at the fleeing men. Regardless, I heard a scream, so perhaps I did hit somebody. Katherine bent down and picked up something that was at her feet. It was a big money roll. Apparently, it had fallen from sarge's pockets during the scuffle. We now had the poker winnings from the night.

I was still shaking as we made our way back to the hotel. We were wary as we walked the streets, looking in every direction to make sure that the men were not following us. We entered our hotel through the back way.

Pelina and Katherine spent the night. I was completely worn out after the scuffle and slept soundly.

July 7, 1867

Sunday breakfast was delivered by room service. It was ham and eggs, waffles, and hot coffee.

We continued to watch the hotel across the street. A little past ten in the morning, we saw the sarge and his companions walking slowly past our hotel. Gus walked with a limp and his lower leg was bandaged. Sarge's arm was also bandaged. It turned out that I wasn't such a terrible shot after all. I had wounded one of them. We got a good look at the men as they walked slowly down the street, and now we could match their names to their faces.

I placed the gun on the table and studied it, then picked it up and turned the cylinder. There were four shots remaining in the chambers.

"What are you going to do with the gun?" Katherine asked.

Pelina giggled. "She could wear it on her waist. Think that it will fit her?"

I stood up and tried the holster on for size. I put it around my waist and threaded the belt through the buckle and pulled it tight. I fastened the prong through the last hole, then placed the gun in its holster.

"It does fit her," Katherine observed.

Pelina seemed intrigued. "Are you going to go out like that, Ginny?"

"Don't you think I look good, Pelina?" I joked.

"Sure, you do, Ginny. Sure as shootin!"

We all laughed. I looked dead serious wearing a gun holster. We needed protection, but a lady carries a gun in her purse, not on a gun belt. That's where I put the gun. We were involved in a dangerous undertaking and a loaded gun was certainly a good precaution.

We continued to observe the hotel across the street for the men. When they did not leave by early afternoon, I decided that we needed to go over and eavesdrop at their door again. I knew that this was risky business, because if they saw us we probably would be dead, but I had to find out more information about their plans.

"May I help you lovely ladies?" The desk clerk at the Garmin Hotel asked as we entered the lobby.

"We are here to visit relatives," I explained.

The clerk smiled and nodded. I am sure that he saw through my fib right away and likely thought that we were just some loose girls there for some quick cash. We climbed the stairs and walked quietly down the second-floor corridor to room number 24. It was quiet inside the room for a while, then we heard the sarge talking.

"Okay, I will be in Newport next week, on Thursday, drivin' the freight wagon. Meet me at the Newport Inn about one in the afternoon."

"Got it sarge," replied one of the men.

Sarge continued. "This is a huge haul of this loot from Georgia, the largest ever."

"I just want this done, sarge. We have been sitting on this too long!"

"Don't worry, Flynt," sarge replied. "We will have a handsome reward in the Cincinnati markets. The loot I'm bringin' in that old wagon is worth a fortune; diamonds, gold, and silver. We're going to be rich, fellas!"

"So… you're bringing the loot in from Frankfort, sarge?"

"Yeah, like I told ya' the other day, that's where the loot is now. I handle that end of the deal. No worries, boys."

There was a long pause.

"So, what's our cut, sarge?"

"Sixty percent!"

"How do we know that, sarge? How do we know if you're not cheating us? I mean, you already come up short here on that money we won last night at the tavern."

Sarge sounded angry. "I have always been on the level with you fellas!"

There was a heated argument and it sounded like it could become violent. We decided that it would be best to leave before heads started to roll.

I had gathered enough information to plan my next move. Back at my room, we discussed everything we had heard.

"They are part of a smuggling ring," Pelina said. "Their contacts are in Frankfort and they're bringing stolen goods north to sell in the black market in Newport."

"They are thieves and murderers," I added. "They stole my father's horses and killed my parents. I haven't any doubt that they have murdered many other innocent people and stolen their property in the Civil War. Now they are selling it and collecting a lot of dirty money."

Katherine pulled out the money roll which she had found last night. "I do not want this!"

She exclaimed with disdain. "I'll have nothing to do with dirty money!"

"We may have to use that money, Katherine." I said. "Sometimes when you're desperate you have to do whatever you can. We have to use that money to get to Newport and stop them."

"How are we going to do that?" Katherine asked.

"I am going to go to the army post in Newport and report them there so that they will be investigated and jailed. Pelina, Katherine, I need your help. So, are you with me in this?"

There was a long silence.

Pelina broke the silence first. "Well, I will have to tell my Ma first. I'll tell her that we're going there for entertainment. Are we getting there by rail or riverboat?"

I thought about it before giving an answer. "I have always wanted to ride on a riverboat, so that would be my first choice."

"Your man friend is on the boat?" Pelina asked.

I shook my head. "No. He's headed to New Orleans and won't be back for many days."

Katherine thought for a moment. "Why don't we take the riverboat there and return on the train?" She suggested.

"How much money is in that roll, Katherine?" I asked. "Did you count it?"

"Not yet…let's count it now and see if we have enough money for the trip."

We counted the money. There were all one-dollar bills in the roll, fifty dollars total. That was more than enough for fare charges, hotels and meals.

We went down to the Cincinnati-Louisville Mail Line ticket office near the landings and purchased our tickets. We bought three cabin fares for ten dollars and fifty cents. We booked on the riverboat steamer The United States, a side wheeler.

We would depart at three o'clock on Tuesday and arrive in Newport on Wednesday morning. This would give me ample time to pay a visit to the provost officer at the Newport Army Barracks.

July 9, 1867

The steamer United States was a fine stately riverboat. Katherine, Pelina and I carried our baggage to the boarding area at the Third Street wharf and waited in line. The big side wheeler, painted all white, was fairly new, and it glistened like a gem in the brilliant mid-afternoon sunshine. Black fumes rose from the two towering smoke stacks in front of the pilot house. We watched as hundreds of barrels of bourbon and gunny sacks of grain were loaded onto the freight deck of the packet boat.

We wore our finest dresses and summer bonnets for this momentous occasion. We could not contain our excitement as we waited to board the majestic river steamer.

Pelina suddenly jabbed me with her elbow. "Look! That man is Flynt!" She gasped.

I looked at the man she pointed to, he was towards the front of the line and he boarded with the second-class passengers onto the freight deck.

"That is Flynt!" I said. "I hope that he didn't see us."

"I don't think that he noticed us in this crowd," Pelina said, reassuringly. Nonetheless, it made me uncomfortable knowing that Flynt was on board. But it did give me some hope that now we could track his movements.

Once the freight was finally loaded the long line of passengers began to move towards the gangway. We walked up the ramp to the main deck and showed our tickets to the clerk. We followed the other first-class passengers up a wide balustraded staircase. This stairway branched halfway up, one stairs curving left and the other right. We moved up the steps to the balcony. Now we found ourselves on the cabin deck. We asked one of the stewards for directions to our room. He said that our state room was on the starboard side and he directed us to the promenade.

"I will show you to your room," he said politely. He took our bags and ushered us to our quarters, unlocked the door and entered, setting our bags on the floor. He inspected the interior, then told us to ring the bell if we needed anything. I thanked him and gave a small tip.

The room was rather narrow, but it was furnished with comfortable chairs, a foldable table on the window wall, and some bunk beds. It was crowded with the three of us, but it was nice to sit at the little window table and look out at the city. We had a good view right up Third Street toward the rows of shops that went onwards up towards Main.

To our right we could see the imposing Louisville Hotel, one of the largest buildings downtown. All along the waterfront were many long-storied warehouses and freight yards. There were many work horses pulling freight wagons back and forth. Louisville was a city hard at work, it never rested.

The whistle sounded several times as the boat shuddered slightly and began moving slowly up river. People waved from the landing and blew kisses as we were under way.

Downtown buildings became smaller as the steamer moved farther out on the river. We passed foundries, mills, factories, and tobacco warehouses along Water Street. I counted the steeples of Louisville's many churches as we went, and I knew all of them by name.

Once we had passed downtown, the residential areas came into view. Two and three story white wood frame houses were just beyond the Fulton Street mills. The windows of homes and factories glittered in the afternoon sunlight as we slowly moved up river. We quickly passed Bear Grass Creek and Butchertown

Our accommodations on The United States were exceptionally grand. We were fortunate to be able to ride in the first-class section. The second class had to ride in very cramped conditions on the freight deck. They had to provide their own meals and bedding. This was an exciting new experience traveling in first class, and I must say, after this, I did not want to go any other way.

About the only advantage the second-class passengers had over first class was that in case the boat was sinking, they could jump off faster from the main deck. But if the boiler blew, as was prone to happening on many an ill-fated riverboat, they would be blown to bits.

We were now passing the outlying areas of Louisville. I recognized the inlet of Harrod's Creek. Memories of my youth flashed by; the horse farm on Mint Spring, the fields where my Papa and I gathered corn, the one room school house where Pelina and I attended several years ago on Wolf Pen Creek. Louisville was quickly fading away in the distance; now we were on our way to new places we had only heard about.

Pelina snapped me out of my reminiscing. "Let's go out and explore the boat!" She suggested.

We went out to the promenade. A steward came and locked our door for us. The promenade was lavishly adorned with an ornate wood carved colonnade with Southern style lattice arches. All the wood was painted white, except for the deck, which was bare.

We walked up the promenade holding our parasols slightly tilted upon our shoulders, trying to imitate the rich ladies on board. There was an open observation deck at the front of the riverboat, with many tables and chairs clustered towards the cabin.

Pelina, Katherine and I sat at one of the tables. This was a nice place to relax and talk. A waiter came and asked us what we would have, so we ordered some drinks. We had some excellent Longworth's Catawba vintage 1863, a famous sparkling wine.

An elegantly dressed young woman holding an umbrella entered from the promenade. She looked at us and smiled. There was an available chair at our table.

I took a sip of wine.

"Mind if I join you?" She inquired.

"Oh, please do," I invited.

"My, aren't you all such lovely young ladies. I've never seen you on board before. Are you looking for prospects?" She giggled.

"Prospects?" I repeated, not really knowing what she meant by that.

She laughed. "Prospects. You know girls, wealthy young men!"

"Oh, yes, we are chasing some men," Pelina volunteered.

"Well, there are many fine eligible bachelors in the first-class section on this steamer, as you will see."

The idea of chasing after a rich boy had never occurred to me, but I am sure that the notion made us most curious. Marrying money and being set for life was an inviting prospect.

"So, girls, tell me your names, and where you are from…"

We introduced one another and told her a little about ourselves. She seemed especially interested when I told her about how Katherine and I had been in an orphanage for several years. She inquired about our parents. She listened intently as I explained how my parents were killed by Union soldiers when I was twelve, and how I was now chasing those same soldiers to Newport. I also told her about the black-market activities which they were operating.

"Please tell us about yourself," I said. "What is your name?"

"I am Theresa Wrampelmeier. My husband is the owner of the Wrampelmeier furniture factory in Louisville. He does a lot of business in Newport and Cincinnati, so we travel the river regularly."

"What kind of furniture do you make at the factory?" Katherine asked.

"We make everything from tables to bedroom furniture to upholstered sofas and chairs. The sofas in the salon area of this boat are made at our Louisville factory. Our products are widely distributed throughout the country."

Mrs. Wrampelmeier paused. I poured her some wine. She smiled and seemed very grateful for the drink.

"John and I came to America from Germany many years ago. We were poor. John learned the furniture business in New York. Then we moved to Louisville and started out in a small warehouse near the river, then we expanded our company. We are now located in our new factory and we've become the largest furniture business in Louisville."

The whistle blew from the uppermost deck. It was very loud. We saw another steamer up river loaded with freight and passengers. It passed us going in the opposite direction and was quickly out of view. We could read the boats name on its paddle wheel housing: The America.

"You all look so very young. What are your ages?" Mrs. Wrampelmeier asked.

"We are seventeen," I replied.

"Oh, my, only seventeen. So young. I am a little more than twice your age…I'm thirty-five."

Pelina seemed surprised. "You are?" I thought that you were twenty!"

Mrs. Wrampelmeier laughed. "No, my dear, I've been around awhile. But many people say that I look much younger than what I actually am. So, have you girls ever been on a riverboat before this trip?"

"This is our first time on a riverboat," I answered. "We've never been out of Jefferson County before. This is all so exciting. I have always wanted to ride on a riverboat since I was nine years old and saw them on the Ohio River. I remember that I was with my Pa on our hay wagon when we went to get supplies at Goose Creek. I'll never forget seeing all the paddle wheelers going up and down the big river."

Mrs. Wrampelmeier smiled. "Now you are on one of the best steamers on the river today. Only the America riverboat is newer. Did you see her? She just went by a minute ago"

"Yes, it looks very much like this boat," I replied.

"Have you been on The America?" Katherine asked.

"Yes. I've been on that boat twice now. It's the largest steamer in the Mail Lines and competes openly with The United States. However, this boat has the best kitchen staff. The chef is the best anywhere."

Mrs. Wrampelmeier looked at her gold brooch watch.

"Dinner will be in about half an hour. Do you girls want to come with me for a tour of the boat, and dine with me and my husband tonight?"

"We would be honored," I said.

We were excited to go on a tour of the boat with Mrs.Wrampelmeier as our guide. She took us to the grand salon, where we stood next to the large brass plated water cooler, gazing in amazement at the expansive hall, about 300 feet long and 40 feet wide. It was lavishly adorned with paneled and frescoed ceilings and soaring gilded lobed arches traversing across the beams. Seven gold plated crystal chandeliers with crimson shades glittered from above. The walls, ceilings, doors and trim all had hand carved exquisite woodwork crafted in many designs. High etched glass windows at the roof line allowed the soft glow of outside light to filter down into the spacious room.

Down the center of the salon dining tables were being readied. Waiters were setting up for dinner, moving chairs to the tables. Silverware, fine porcelain dishes and crystal glassware were set in place.

Rows of doors on each side of the magnificent length of the salon led to the state rooms.

"At the other end is the ladies' salon," Mrs. Wrampelmeier told us. "The other door of your state room will open to this section, also. Have you found the baths?"

"No, we haven't been there yet." I said.

"Just follow me, my dears. You must know where the baths are located."

We followed Mrs. Wrampelmeier down to the ladies' section. There was a huge ceiling high mirror here with doors to each side. A variety of plants had been placed along the wall lattice, and the foliage draped down from above.

We went into the ladies' wash room. There were several private bath chambers where ladies might have warm baths with mineral salts. There was also a long counter with built in sinks and running water taps…a real luxury for those times. A line of women waited with number chips for their turn to take a bath. Maids scurried around to wait on the needs of the women in the wash room. It was a busy atmosphere in there. Soaps, shampoos, mineral oils and towels were provided by the maids. Manicures and hair styling services were also available, and several ladies sitting on plush sofas were availing themselves of such treatments.

I wanted to try the baths and hair styling, but this was a short trip and it was almost time eat. I was more eager for dinner to begin at the moment. Pelina could give us a quick makeover in our state room.

Mrs. Wrampelmeier also showed us the bridal suites, child care center, and the upper balcony area with the crew cabins and pilot house. The views were inspiring from the upper deck, often called the Texas. We stood next to the imposing black smoke stacks looking at both shores of the wide river; there was mostly woods dotted with farmland and a few small towns.

We could hear the grand piano down below from the salon. A catchy tune was being played to signal the start of dinner. We descended the stairs back to the cabin deck. Upon entering the dining area, we saw many of the first-class travelers leaving their state rooms and finding a place at one of the many tables. The pianist continued to play tunes as the passengers waited to place orders.

The gas lighted chandeliers made the big room bright and cheerful. We selected a table toward the upper end of the salon and sat down. Mrs. Wrampelmeier saw her husband in the crowd and she whistled and motioned for him to come and join us. He took off his black silk top hat and placed it on a hat rack near a wide doorway, then he came and sat down next to his wife.

"So, what's for dinner tonight, dear?" He asked. He gave us a quick glance. "I see that you have met some new friends here."

"Yes, these young ladies are on their first river trip and I have been giving them a proper orientation of the first-class accommodations. Oh, let me introduce you…girls, this is my husband, Mr. Wrampelmeier."

Mrs. Wrampelmeier then introduced us one at a time as her husband kissed our hands and said our names.

"You look so very young!" He exclaimed.

"They are all only seventeen." Mrs. Wrampelmeier said.

Mr. Wrampelmeier shook his head and smiled. "So, this is your first trip on a riverboat? Well, you will absolutely love this one. She's only two years old, built in Cincinnati in 1865 by the U.S. Mail Line Company. Their newest sidewheeler, The America, was launched earlier this year. So, we have The United States and The America operated by the same company, both assigned to serve the Louisville – Cincinnati route."

"I think that this is the best way to travel," I commented. "I would like to visit other cities like St. Louis or New Orleans and go by riverboat."

"Well, just let me know if you do…I can recommend the best boats that go to those places."

Night on a Riverboat

The waiter came to take our order. We each had a menu on the table in front of us, but I was having a difficult time deciding what to get. There were so many selections from which to choose. The menu was listed by categories: Beef dishes, Fowl, Pork, Mutton, Sea Food, Desserts, and Beverages.

Mr. and Mrs. Wrampelmeier recommended the roast duck. We all ordered that, and we were not disappointed. It was the best I've ever had, served with mashed potatoes and gravy with string beans and a side salad. For drink, we had an excellent wine that Mr. Wrampelmeier ordered. It was a feast for nobility.

"So, all you young ladies are from Louisville?" Mr. Wrampelmeier asked.

"Pelina and I grew up on farms outside of Louisville, near Harrods Creek," I explained. "Katherine is from Louisville."

"Ginny and I have been closest friends since first grade at Wolf Pen School," Pelina said. "I still live on the farm, my family owns a lot of acreage by Mint Creek, not far from Ginny's place…I mean, where she grew up. She lives in Louisville now."

Mrs. Wrampelmeier looked at Katherine, "You haven't said much about yourself, dear."

Katherine smiled. "I have lived in Louisville all my life. My Ma died when I was six and I never had a Pa. I grew up in the orphanage…St. Vincent's in Louisville. That's where Ginny and I met after her parents were murdered."

"Your parents were murdered?" Mr. Wrampelmeier said, giving me a concerned look.

I told him about that fateful day in 1862 when my Mama and Papa were murdered by the soldiers. Mr. Wrampelmeier shook his head in disbelief and expressed disgust.

Then I told him about how we were following the same soldiers who had committed this violent act. "The sarge is the man who actually killed my Mama and Papa. So, he is the one that I want to get the most. The other men were with him when he did it. One of those soldiers is on this boat!"

Mr. Wrampelmeier looked shocked. "Where is he?"

"He's on the main deck in second class. We saw him getting on, but he did not see us."

I continued. "We overheard the sarge saying that he was going to meet his companions in Newport, and he also said that he was bringing some loot in a freight wagon from Frankfort. Apparently, this "loot" is diamonds, gold and silver that was plundered from homes in the South at the end of the war."

Mr. Wramplemeier took his last bite of roast duck and wiped his mouth and thick moustache with a cloth napkin. He heaved a deep sigh.

"Ginny, I think that you may be in over your head. How do you intend to stop these criminals?"

"I intend to use whatever legal means I can…the police or the army provost at Newport Barracks."

"That will be difficult; many of these kinds of criminal activities go unpunished and law enforcement winks an eye."

"Well, I will find a way. If the police do nothing I will take matters into my own hands. I am going to make sure that sarge pays for what he did to my parents."

The Wrampelmeier's both nodded but they looked rather uncomfortable with my suggestion of taking personal vengeance. If frontier justice was the only way, then so be it, one way or another, the sarge had to pay for his war crimes.

"Let me know how it goes with the authorities, Ginny." Mr Wrampelmeier smiled. "I have some friends in high places in Newport, I may be able to help."

"Thank you, sir."

Mr. Wrampelmeier reached into his overcoat and pulled out some business cards. He handed them to me.

"My Newport office is printed on that first card. The other one has the address of our showroom in Louisville. We have jobs available at our Fourth Street showroom if you would like to work for us."

"I would be honored to work for you. I will give your kind offer consideration," I replied.

We finished our meal and continued to make good conversation while we sipped our wine. We probably had too much wine, as we were becoming quite giddy. I had more to drink than anyone else.

When I rose from my chair to go to the washroom, I fell to the floor. I rolled around laughing hysterically. Pelina and Katherine tried to pick me up, but they couldn't.

"Oh, my, she doesn't hold her liquor well," Mrs. Wrampelmeier said, quite alarmed.

"I should have stopped her, she was drinking down that wine like it was water," Mr. Wrampelmeier exclaimed.

I stood up and started to run about the dining area, laughing and knocking against tables, spilling drinks all over the place. I glided over to a table of nice looking young men, and I sat on their laps and started to kiss them.

Pelina came over and slapped my face, then she and Katherine pulled me off the men and assisted me back to our state room. They forced me to lay down on my bed, but I kept laughing and kicking my legs, trying to get up. Pelina shook me and shouted at me to be still. I stopped wiggling and stared up at Pelina's face; then I passed out.

When I woke up it was dark in the room, and I was alone. A little bit of light entered the room from a small window above the door. I could hear clapping and cheering coming from the salon. I wondered what was going on, and I became angry that I was not included. I looked at my brooch watch that Walter had given me. It was nearing 10 o'clock.

I got up and turned the gas light knob so that it lit from the pilot. I looked at myself in the mirror a brushed my hair and sprayed on some perfume. I opened the door and stepped into the ladies' salon area. A steward locked the state room door behind me. I looked everywhere in the ladies' section for Pelina and Katherine, but I did not see them. I could hear some kind of show going on in the main salon, so I went that way to find out what was going on in that section of the riverboat.

Some of the ladies gave me some hard stares, apparently showing their aversion to my drunken behavior at dinner. I barely remembered what I had done, it now seemed like a bad dream. I was embarrassed by the stares.

I entered the main salon. Some men began to cluster around me and made aggressive remarks and gestures. One of the men tried to pin me against the wall. A swift kick to his lower extremities made all the men back away and leave, laughing as they went, their friend doubled over in pain.

There were some circus performers doing an act with unicycles on a tightwire, juggling and blowing flames from their mouths. All the tables had been moved to the side and the chairs were placed in rows for the passengers. I went over to where the spectators were enjoying the show and looked for Pelina and Katherine.

I watched the acrobats for a while, admiring their exceptional performance. It was incredible to see them juggle pins while moving across the high wire on a unicycle, it took incredible balance and skill to accomplish these feats.

I heard some banjo music coming from the front deck. I decided to go there and search for Pelina and Katherine.

I walked up the promenade to the observation deck, where we had met Mrs. Wrampelmeier earlier. There was a crowd of passengers here now; some playing cards at tables, others watching, and many more were singing and clapping to the banjo and fiddle music. Drinks were flying from the bar room at a furious pace.

I pushed through the crowd looking for Pelina and Katherine. There were some people dancing in the thick of everything, and that's where I found them; dancing with many partners. I was thinking that it was confounded obvious that they had too much to drink by now, as they were being excessively silly. I was grabbed by some men and forced out to the dance floor. I really did not care to dance but by that time I had no choice but to join the festivities.

I started to enjoy myself. The dancing was not like some boring ball room type that was going on in the main salon with the conclusion of the show. Couples were doing a variation of some folk dances, changing partners often. It was a fun lively dance with a lot of turning and kicking with very energetic movements that kept pace with the quick tempo of the banjo and fiddle.

We danced so much that we began to get worn out. I stopped first, then Katherine and finally Pelina. We stood at the bar, and several men offered us drinks, but we refused.

We saw some of the other girls getting ice cream. That was a treat that we did not have very often; I only tried it once before at the state fair. The ice cream here was so cold and smooth, served in a parfait glass with a cherry on top. We sat on some bar style stools as we enjoyed the delicious ice cream treat.

A commotion suddenly erupted from one of the card tables. There was Flynt in the middle of it! He stood up and drew his gun. A man on the opposite side of the table jumped to his feet and also drew his revolver.

"It's Flynt!" Pelina cried out. "What's he doing up here?"

"Looks like he sneaked up here to get into the high stakes card games," Katherine said.

"He's a cheat!" Yelled the man "Nothin' but a dirty filthy scoundrel! He loaded the deck, saw him do it…"

"Yeah, no wonder he's cleanin' everybody out!" Yelled another.

Flynt grabbed the pile of money and started to retreat from the table. Two burly stewards came and grabbed him on each arm.

"Put the money down!" One of them ordered.

Flynt threw the money back down on the table. The stewards searched through Flynt's pockets and pulled out his boarding ticket.

"Alright, you've a second-class ticket, mate. You don't belong here. Got a mind to throw you overboard!"

They started to carry Flynt to the railing and I thought they were going to do it. They dangled him upside down over the tail. Flynt screamed out for help, but all the onlookers just laughed.

"Throw him overboard! Throw him overboard!" They jeered.

I gasped at this prospect. If Flynt were thrown overboard, I would certainly lose my advantage of being able to track him and the sarge once we got to Newport.

At the last moment they pulled him back up to the deck and pushed him down, punched and kicked him several times, then they horse collared him and dragged him down the stairs to the freight deck.

I was relieved that he wasn't thrown overboard. One thing for sure, he got what he deserved; he had that coming for a long time. But if he had gone overboard my plans would have gone awry.

We finished our ice cream. It was almost midnight. The bell on the top deck was ringing loud and clear, sending out a signal to another river vessel in the night, indicating our location.

It was late, and we would be docking in Newport very early Wednesday morning.

We returned to the main salon, where an orchestra was playing on into the night. Several couples were dancing and at the other side people sat at tables enjoying drinks. We watched the dancing for a while, then returned to our state room.

We played checkers and chatted until half past one in the morning. Katherine won all the games as she always did.

We slept soundly through the night. In the morning we took a very relaxing bath in scented oils, had our hair styled, and then a breakfast of biscuits, ham and eggs.

July 10, 1867

We returned to our state room to get ready to leave. I opened the curtains to our stateroom window and was surprised to see many imposing buildings outside.

"I thought that we were in Newport!" I exclaimed.

Katherine came over and peered out the window. "I don't think this is Newport…it must be Cincinnati."

Pelina joined us at the window. "Yeah, look at all the hogs being unloaded. This is Cincinnati alright. We're in Porkopolis."

We packed our bags and went out onto the promenade. There was a negro steward on duty and I asked him for information.

"Are we in Cincinnati?"

"Yes ma'am, we are indeed in Cincinnati, at the Vine Street wharf."

"We wanted to get off in Newport."

"It will be twelve hours before we arrive there. We have to unload and load freight first. Most everyone takes the Newport ferry from Lawrence Street."

The friendly steward explained to us how to get to the Newport ferry, but we did not really understand the directions. When we got off the boat we were completely confused and lost.

Arrival

Getting lost in The Queen City was not such a bad thing. We walked around the business district, visiting many shops along Vine Street and Walnut. I purchased some imported teas at a variety store. We also bought scented soaps and perfumes at some specialty shops. The streets were crowded with shoppers even though it was only the middle of the week. Cincinnati was very impressive with row upon row of brick masonry buildings with fine ornamental crown ledges adorning windows and rooftops.

It was a fascinating city to explore. We would have stayed longer, but I felt the need to get to our destination.

We had to ask again for directions to the ferry. A nice gentleman showed us to Front Street and pointed us in the right direction.

"Thank you, sir," I said. "We have been lost all morning!"

"Everybody gets lost here," he said with a wink. "And before you know it, you've spent all your life and fortune in this place."

We went down Front Street and found Lawrence, then turned right towards the ferry berth.

We paid our two-cent fare and went up a wide ramp to the ferry deck and sat down on a wooden bench. Many people crowded onto the small stern-wheeler until there was no more room. There was a greasy odor here, probably from all the industry situated along the river.

As we approached the ferry landings on the Newport side of the river, I saw the Wrampelmeiers. When we got off the ferry Mrs. Wrampelmeier waved at us.

"Oh, there you are!" She greeted. "Sorry we missed you this morning. We had to take care of some business today."

"Thank you for waiting for us." I said.

"Oh, no bother at all, we were just leaving the bank and I told John that we should come to the ferry port and see if we might join up with you girls."

"We got lost in Cincinnati and spent a lot of time in some of the stores over there," I explained.

"Well, it's easy to lose one self in Cincinnati," she laughed. "Come, girls, we have a coach waiting over there."

It was beyond my expectations that we would receive such a wonderful welcome in Newport. The Wrampelmeiers knew the town well and they showed us around. Newport was a vibrant community with many diversions. The coach finally stopped in front of a hotel.

"This is the nicest place to stay here in Newport," Mr. Wrampelmeier told us. "This is the Frontier Inn. I highly recommend it."

"How much is it here a night?" I asked.

"They have some rooms available for just a half dollar a day."

We checked in and moved into a spacious room on the second floor. We rested for about half an hour, then I read a Cincinnati newspaper that I had bought in the city.

There was a knock at the door. Katherine opened it and a steward delivered a message from the Wrampelmeier's inviting us to lunch at noon.

We went to a German restaurant on Monmouth Street. I had some delicious beef stroganoff. It was the best I've ever eaten, authentic from the Old World. I remembered that my Ma's best recipes were from the Old world. This brought back good memories of when my parents were alive.

"Ginny, I have something to tell you," Mr. Wrampelmeier said as he finished his main course. "The police inspector here is a friend of mine. I spoke to him this morning about your situation with sarge. He has assured me that he will alert his men about their scheme, and they will make an attempt to intercept the freight wagon."

I was overjoyed that there was finally some good news. "Thank you, Mr. Wrampelmeier. I sincerely hope that they will catch them, and they get what they deserve. They need to be locked up so that they will not hurt anyone else."

Mr. Wrampelmeier nodded. "There are some legal statutes on the books that apply to this case. I assume that they will be prosecuted to the fullest extent of the law if they are caught with the stolen goods."

"I was going to see the provost officer at the Newport Army Barracks today. Do you think that I should still go?" I asked.

"Yes, by all means, do. This is still an army issue. I would check there and see if they can offer any assistance. At lease file a report in the matter, so that an investigation might be initiated."

"Okay, I will go there after lunch."

Mr. Wrampelmeier gave me directions to the army post. I left right away. Pelina and Katherine came with me. We walked up Taylor Street through the center of Newport. We passed an open-air market, a gun shop, and a few jewelry stores.

The clock on the town hall showed ten minutes past one. The stores in town were not busy at his hour.

We passed some row housing on the west side of town as we approached the barracks. We entered at the Central Street visitors gate. There were several colonial type buildings along a central park like area. We went directly to the headquarters building. A guard greeted us in a spacious lobby.

"May I help you ladies?" He inquired.

"We want to speak to the provost officer," I replied.

"The provost marshal's office is across the green, in the auxiliary building. Just go around the circle to the other side."

I thanked the guard and we headed to the circular walk that went around the grassy, tree lined green which gave an arboreal appearance to the army post. We found the building easily and entered a wide colonnaded porch, where the door stood wide open. We went inside.

It was confusing to find our way in the auxiliary building. There were many different offices there. We finally found the office of the army provost and entered a small reception area.

An overweight staff officer greeted us. "May I help you, ma'am?"

"Yes," I replied. "I would like to file a report about a crime committed by some soldiers."

"You will have to complete an official form called a criminal investigation report bofore it will be reviewed by this office."

"Okay, give me the form. I will fill it out now."

I filled out the report. It took a long time to describe the incidents of criminal activity. I reported my parents' murder and the illegal activities in which the sarge and the others were now engaged. When I was finished with the report, I handed it to the staff officer. He read it over closely, frowned, and looked up at me.

"I will submit your report to our investigations department. You should hear back from us soon. Where may we contact you?"

I gave him the address of our hotel.

As we were leaving the building we saw a group of soldiers walking toward us. We froze in our tracks. Gus and Flynt were there! We abruptly turned and started to walk briskly towards the main gate. We opened our parasols and covered our faces.

Several of the men spotted us and they cat whistled. They laughed and snickered at us loudly, making rude remarks. We got out of there just in time.

We took a coach back to our hotel. I was not feeling well after the close encounter at the army post. At least I had accomplished what I had set out to do there when we left this morning.

I rested in my comfortable bed until it was time for dinner. We decided to order room service. The hotel restaurant brought us some excellent roast beef and poultry dishes along with black eyed peas smothered in bacon.

After our meal we took a walk-up Monmouth Street and shopped at some ladies' apparel stores but did not buy anything. Later we discovered several taverns and gambling halls near the river.

Lamplighters were out, lighting up the town's gas lamps as evening settled upon Newport. The taverns looked inviting, so we went into one of the larger ones and sat down at a table. We ordered some red wine along with some ham and cheese on crackers.

We left the tavern early. I wanted to get a good night's sleep because I knew that tomorrow would be a busy day. I did not want to over indulge in the wine either, as I had done on the riverboat journey.

Back at the hotel room we read the advertisements in the Cincinnati Enquirer newspaper, played a few rounds of skat, then went to bed by eleven o'clock.

July 11, 1867

The next morning, we had our bath and breakfast at the hotel. We sent our clothes out to be laundered so we had to wait most of the morning for them to be cleaned and delivered back to our room.

We left the hotel at eleven o'clock, searching for the Newport Inn. That is where sarge said that he would meet his friends at one o'clock. We learned that the Newport Inn was on Columbia Street. We walked there and stood in front of the small hotel. There was a restaurant directly across the street. We decided to return later and have lunch at this restaurant, so we would have a good view of the hotel.

After spending some time at an open-air market near the town hall, where I bought some fresh fruits and peanuts, we rushed back to the restaurant, arriving just before one o'clock.

We entered the restaurant and requested a table by the front window and placed our order. I had just finished my bowl of hot chowder when I saw Gus, Josh and Flynt standing across the street.

"There they are!" I exclaimed.

The three men were in front of the hotel, nervously glancing up the street, undoubtedly looking for the sarge.

A carriage pulled up in front of the hotel. For a few anxious moments we could not see the men. When the carriage pulled away, sarge was standing next to them. He held a small carrying case.

"What do you suppose is in that case?" Pelina asked, looking rather puzzled.

I did not reply immediately. I was bewildered that sarge did not arrive in his freight wagon. Apparently, he had left the freight wagon somewhere else and already had sold the loot.

I knew what this meant. "It looks like he has sold the loot already and that would certainly mean that he's got the money in that carrying case," I said, looking at Pelina. "Is that what you are thinking, too?"

She nodded in agreement. My plan of catching sarge with the loot in his possession as indisputable evidence had completely failed. I felt desperation and anguish like I had just been run over by a freight train. It was futile now, how would I ever get justice served against these men? I considered the loaded gun in my hand bag. Four bullets, four men…

I could do it. I could walk out there and shoot them dead in the street. Of course, I would hang for my actions. But that's a sacrifice that I was ready to make.

I felt for the gun in my handbag. I felt the barrel with my fingertips as I stood, looking at sarge and his friends across the street.

"Ginny, what are you doing?" Katherine exclaimed.

"I'm going to put an end to this once and for all!" I shouted.

I grabbed my handbag and ran towards the door. Katherine and Pelina rushed forward and held me back. "Let me go!" I yelled.

"No, Ginny, stop! Let's go sit down and talk this over," Pelina said. "Ginny…now! Sit back down!"

Pelina and Katherine grabbed my arms and forced me back to my seat. I looked across the street. Sarge and the others had left.

"Look! They're gone!" I shouted. "Those evil men will pay for what they did to my parents! They will die! They will! They will! I will kill them!"

I hid my face in my hands and wailed.

The waiter came over and told us to leave. Katherine became angry and yelled at him.

"Can't you understand that we are just trying to help our friend?" She screamed, her face getting red.

"I will summon the police!" He bellowed.

"Go ahead!" Katherine shot back.

He promptly went out to the street and turned the hand crank on the police alarm box. It's loud ring echoed in all directions. Several police whistles sounded, growing louder as the officers ran towards the alarm.

We ran from the restaurant just in time to see sarge and his companions running in the opposite direction. They had not left after all but were standing back in a corner or alley somewhere, undoubtedly conducting business.

Three policemen came and started chasing sarge and his accomplices. Sarge tripped and fell face down on the sidewalk, dropping the carrying case. It slid beyond his reach. Flynt grabbed it and ran. He, Gus and Josh got away, but they caught sarge and handcuffed him.

The waiter seemed content that we were out of his restaurant. He returned to his work. Sarge was hauled off to jail.

We returned to the hotel and discussed the day's turn of events. I decided that we needed to visit the police headquarters and find out what was going to happen with sarge.

The police chief would not provide us with very much information that was worthwhile. We left with the impression that he would be held for interrogation and then probably released.

We had dinner at another outstanding restaurant on Monmouth Street. Mr. Wrampelmeier told me after our meal that the sarge was able to evade the police by arriving early in the pre-dawn hours. He made a delivery at a foundry on the outskirts of Newport where he left the freight wagon. Mr. Wrampelmeier suspected that the sarge was paid some big cash for the stolen goods somewhere near the foundry; or at the foundry grounds. The foundry was near the river, so the stolen goods could easily have been smuggled across to Cincinnati. It would have been partitioned there, making the loot untraceable.

Back at our hotel room I was not feeling well. It seemed like all my efforts to get justice done was a waste of time. I laid in my bed staring at the ceiling, wondering what I could possibly do now to obtain justice. It seemed like the only way to stop these men was to fight them myself. I still had a loaded gun in my handbag.

As twilight approached Pelina suggested that we go to the tavern that we had visited last night. I really wasn't feeling up to it, but a few drinks might be just what I needed to feel better and forget my troubles.

We dressed elegantly for a night out on the town, then departed the hotel and headed up Monmouth Street. The restaurants, taverns, and gaming halls were becoming crowded early. We passed the magic glow of many street lamps as we made our way to the tavern.

We sat at the same table as last night and ordered a bottle of fine Catawba wine, brewed in the area. I sipped at the wine, enjoying its natural rich aroma and flavor.

Pelina and Katherine were out on the dance floor almost at once, having a wonderful time. I continued to sip my wine, watching the dancers out on the floor.

One of the women dancers looked very familiar. I was sure that she was someone I knew, but at first, I could not quite recognize her. I stared at her for a long time. She was very attractive and a good dancer; indubitably enjoying herself in the midst of many men, laughing and dancing with many different partners, lifting her dress and showing off her petticoats.

It suddenly occurred to me that this woman was Nellie Belle, my Uncle's wife! What was she doing here? I began to wonder if she really was Nellie Belle, or just someone who was a close resemblance.

There was a break in the music and Pelina and Katherine sat down. They had to refuse the advances of many drunken men.

The woman that I had pegged as Nellie Belle came directly towards our table with a troop of men. I decided to find out if she was indeed Nellie Belle.

"Nellie Belle!" I shouted over the loud noise of the crowd. "Nellie Belle, is that you?"

She immediately wheeled around and faced me. She recognized me right away and looked very surprised.

"Ginny! Lands sake, girl, what are you doing here!"

"That's funny, Nellie Belle, I was just about to ask you the same question," I replied, feeling uncomfortable with the presence of my Uncle's wife in a tavern almost a hundred miles from home. She looked young and stunningly beautiful in her elegant French bustle dress.

She laughed. "Well, I asked you first…"

"I am here to get the man who murdered my parents," I said matter-of-factly.

"So, you know who this person is?" She asked with a bewildered look written on her face.

"Yes, I do, and he's here in Newport…"

Nellie Belle pulled up a chair and sat down next to me.

"Who is this man?"

"His men call him sarge. We have chased him and his friends here all the way from Louisville. They are all a bunch of rotten apples, profiting from stolen goods from the Civil War."

"Did you report them to the police?"

"Yes. But the police have done nothing," I replied.

"So, are you sure these men are the murderers?"

"Yes, absolutely. I overheard them talking about killing my folks in their hotel room in Louisville."

I took a long gulp of wine. Nellie Belle was silent, as though she were searching for words.

"So, what are you doing here, Nellie Belle?"

She let out another long laugh. "I got to go somewhere, Ginny. Your Uncle done kicked me out and is filing for a divorce. He's running out of money and in bad debt. I had to get away. He got real mean and was threatening to shoot me…"

I did not know what to make of this. I knew that Nellie Belle tended to sway the truth at every turn to her own advantage. But I also knew that she and my Uncle were not getting along since just before the time I had left home.

"So, I guess that's it then, Nellie Belle," I said. "You and my Uncle are through."

"Well, it's like I said, Ginny. He kicked me out for good. He's not the same man as before. That marriage is over."

"I see. So now you are out looking for another relationship?"

"Yes, Ginny. I am only twenty-three. The men all still find me irresistible, so I will play them for all they're worth. I can pull them in by the ear."

I raised my eyebrows. Of course, at this point I was thinking that this is exactly what she did with my Uncle.

"How long have you been in Newport?" Katherine asked politely.

"Almost two weeks now. I'm starting to get bored here, though. I may hop on a riverboat and head to St. Louis in a few days, then go to visit my folks in Memphis."

"You are from Memphis?" Katherine inquired.

"Yes. I grew up near there on a farm. My pappy grows tobacco and other crops. They just barely make ends meet with eight children including myself."

Katherine continued her questions. "How are you traveling, by boat or railroad?"

"We're taking a riverboat, of course. The train is cramped and hot this time of year. The riverboats are the most entertaining way to go; great food, dancing, games, shows. Everything a woman like me could ask for. The railroads don't hold a candle to going first class on the riverboats."

"You said "we're taking a riverboat."" I said with a hint of scrutiny in my tone. "Who are you going with?"

"I'm going with my new boyfriend," she responded with an almost poisonous smirk.

"Oh…and who is he?" I asked.

"I met him here on Wednesday night."

"Wednesday night?" Pelina said as she poured another glass of wine. "We were here then, but we left early."

"Really? I got here a little late, about ten. We must have just missed each other then."

"So, Nellie Belle, tell us about your new boyfriend, we're just dying to hear about him," I said, rolling my eyes.

"He's a soldier, stationed here at the army barracks. He got lots of money, too. He was buying rounds of drinks for everybody and he gave me some jewelry, see my new gold bracelet? He said that he's going to be rich from a certain business deal that is going down today. Don't know much about that. I'm supposed to meet him here tonight though and he's going to give me more money for our trip."

"What is his name?" I inquired.

She looked away with a smirk on her face. I forced a smile as I looked straight into her eyes. "Nellie Belle, you didn't answer my question. What is his name?"

"His name is Flynt. He's going to take me to St. Louis on Saturday morning."

"Why are you glaring at me, Ginny?" Nellie Belle quipped, appearing somewhat agitated. "Oh, Ginny, you look so serious. We should be having fun and merriment, you need to lighten up, girl!"

"Does this Flynt have wavy brown hair and a scar on his right temple?" I asked dryly.

"Why, yes he does! He said that he got that scar in the final battle of the Civil War. It sounds as though you know him."

"Yes, I do. He's a criminal, a real scoundrel."

Nellie Belle's face reddened. "How do you know that?"

"We followed him up here from Louisville. He's a card sharp and…"

Nellie Belle cut me short. "Oh, that's not so bad, Ginny. Sometimes you have to accept people as they are. All the soldiers that fought in the Civil War are gamblers, heavy drinkers, and gun slingers…but Flynt has a certain charm and wit about him that I like. He treats me good."

"Listen to me, Nellie Belle, you are making a big mistake. I know Flynt and I know how he got that money…"

Nellie Belle let out another boisterous laugh. "Ginny, you don't know the first thing about men…I've been with scores of them and I know how to handle them. I've been around, honey, and I don't need advice from a little Miss prim and proper like you."

"I'm tired of you always treating me like a little girl, Nellie Belle. I find your behavior and demeanor to be very immature. If you don't want to listen to me then when the roof falls in I'm not going to say I told you so."

"You are becoming very pushy there, girl…"

I grimaced and gave her a mean look. "Well, you're one to talk, Nellie Belle, after pushing me out of my own house!"

I could sense that she was becoming angry. "Ginny, I have always treated you with the utmost respect. I pushed you out so that you could become independent and to make your own decisions. I see how little you have grown up."

"You pushed me out of my own home and off the farm so that you could have it for yourself!"

Nellie Belle rolled her eyes and looked away. "You are way too serious for me...I'm here to have a good time...Nice seeing you Ginny."

Nellie Belle got up suddenly and went prancing back out to the dance floor. She was laughing and having a great time swinging around and showing off her colorful petticoats.

"What are we going to do, Ginny?" Pelina asked with a worried expression.

I thought for a moment. "We could wait here and see what happens, like we did at the tavern in Louisville the night when we were chased down Market Street."

"If you want we will stay awhile. I don't think that Flynt ever did get a good look at us, even when we were at the tavern in Louisville," Pelina replied.

"Yeah. I don't think he's going to recognize us," Katherine added. "But just in case..." She reached into her handbag. "Here are some Chinese hand fans."

We continued to slowly sip our wine. I had learned on the riverboat to drink in moderation. I could not afford public drunkenness tonight.

At around 11:30, Flynt walked into the barroom. He was dressed in a nice tailored black dress-coat with vest, gold watch, and long trousers. He looked like a refined gentleman.

He did not even notice us sitting at the table. Nellie Belle saw that he and arrived and immediately went and grabbed him by the arm and pulled him out to the dance floor.

They danced for a long time and then they had several drinks. They stood over by the bar and talked, laughing and chugging down one drink after another.

Nellie Belle suddenly pointed at us and giggled as she said something. Flynt looked at us. We held the Chinese fans up in front of our faces. He stared at us with a very stern look.

"Do you think we should get out of here?" Katherine said, nervously glancing at me.

"Wait!" I implored. "We do not wish to cause a stir."

Flynt and Nellie Belle walked towards our table. She held onto his arm.

"Girls!" She proclaimed. "Here is the man I've been tellin' you about. This is Flynt. So, what do you all think?"

We nodded and forced an uncomfortable smile.

"Aint he just the best lookin' gentleman you ever did see, girls?"

"Yes, Nellie Belle, you sure know how to pick 'em," I replied.

Flynt stared at me. "You seem familiar," he said. "In fact, I think that I've seen all of you girls somewhere before."

There was a short pause in the conversation.

"They're all from around Louisville," Nellie Belle replied with a laugh.

My knees were shaking. I took a long sip of wine and looked away from Flynt. I was afraid to say anything, Flynt continued to scrutinize us with an icy glare.

"I know that I've seen you girls somewhere, not that long ago. Say, aren't you those three girls that was… uh"

"Oh, Flynt, how would you know these girls? They do not know you, either! They're only seventeen!" Nellie Belle laughed and grabbed onto his arm again, pulling him away from our table, as though she were keeping him from us. She whispered something in his ear; then he nodded and smiled.

They left the barroom very drunk and happy, headed for a nearby hotel.

We finished our wine and were about to leave when we heard several gunshots from the street.

Most of the patrons in the tavern continued what they were doing as though nothing had happened. Pelina, Katherine and I ran outside to see what the commotion was. Several policemen were pushing their way through the crowd, blowing their whistles.

Flynt lay in the street, crying out in agony as blood rushed from his chest. Nellie Belle knelt at his side, screaming for help.

Sarge laid in a pool of blood about four feet away, moaning with a bullet in his gut.

The police looked at the wounded men. "Go get Doc Fletcher, hurry!" One of the policemen commanded.

Doc Fletcher was summoned from his home. When he arrived, he declared Flynt as dead. Nellie Belle became hysterical, wailing over his lifeless body. I went over to comfort her, and she cried in my arms. Doc attended to sarge's wounds, dressing them with bandages from his medical kit. A hospital team arrived in a transport wagon. They placed sarge on a stretcher and hauled him off to the nearby hospital. Another wagon arrived from the coroner's office, and they carted off Flynt's body to the mortuary.

I walked Nellie Belle back to her hotel room. Pelina and Katherine returned to the Frontier Inn. I spent the night comforting Nellie Belle. She was distraught for hours into the night. I really felt bad for her.

I was awakened in the morning by loud pounding at the door. I got up and was about to open it, but then I decided that it would be best to keep it locked.

"Who's there?" I shouted.

There was some hesitation as though someone was thinking about what to say. "Front desk," a man's raspy voice rang out. "You need to settle your tab now or leave immediately!"

"Nellie Belle," I exclaimed. "Do you owe money for the room?"

Nellie Belle rolled over in bed and mumbled "open it."

I opened the door. Gus and Josh burst into the room.

"What do you think you're doing!" I screamed, then Gus belted me with his fist on the side of the head.

"Where's the money?" Gus demanded.

Nellie Belle bolted to her feet in alarm. "What money?" Gus slapped her across the face.

"Leave her alone!" I demanded. My challenge was met with another blow to the cheek.

"You know what money, you ratbags!" He pushed Nellie Belle back onto the bed. I watched in horror as they ransacked the room. Then they yanked Nellie Belle off the bed and tore open the mattress and pillows.

When they did not find the money, they grabbed Nellie Belle and slapped her again and again.

"Stop it!" I yelled.

Josh slapped me so hard that I fell to the floor. I screamed out in anguish.

"There's no money here, Josh. It's probably back in Flynt's room."

Gus yanked Nellie Belle's hair back. "Tell us where the room is or we're going to kill both of you right now. Where is it?"

Gus brandished a revolver and held it to her head. Do you got a key for Flynt's room? Huh? Where was he staying?"

"Please! I don't know. Please don't kill me!" Nellie Belle pleaded.

"On, no? Josh, search her handbag."

Josh dumped the contents of Nellie Belle's handbag out onto the floor. Her makeup, combs and brushes scattered in all directions. Josh found six dollars in her wallet and he took it. But there was no room key.

Gus looked very angry. His face turned red. He ordered us to our feet and told us to get dressed. We were still in our night gowns.

"Gus, look, they're both bleeding bad." Josh said. "We can't leave here with 'em lookin' like that."

"Yeah, I guess you're right, Josh. Guess we'll have to deal with them here. Well, I'm just going to have to get them to talk, what are they hiding? Did you find any clues in her handbag?"

"It looks like a note there. I don't know, Gus."

Gus looked down at the floor. "Well, what do we have here?" He reached down and picked up a piece of paper that had fallen out of Nellie Belle's handbag.

"What's this?" He unfolded the piece of paper. There was an address written on it. "What's this address here?" He demanded, looking at Nellie Belle. "You tell me what I need to know about this address or I'll start breakin' some bones, starting with your wrist and then your neck!"

He grabbed Nellie Belle again and started to twist her wrist. She cried out in pain.

"Please, stop! I'll tell you what you want to know. Please stop!"

Nellie Belle winced in pain as he twisted her arm behind her back. "Tell me whose address this is!"

"Okay, I'll talk. Please, let go of my arm! You're hurting me!"

"Alright, then, are you going to tell us what we need to know?"

He let go of her arm. "Talk!"

"It's the address of the boarding house where Flynt was staying…"

Gus pushed her against the wall. "So, this is the address where Flynt was staying. This boarding house on Tenth Street…and that's where the money is. We'll go there and break in the door and take it."

"What are we going to do with them?" Josh asked with a puzzled look.

"We shoot 'em."

Gus raised his gun and pointed it at Nellie Belle. She cringed in fear.

Josh looked concerned. "The shots would be heard a block away. We'd be caught for sure."

Gus thought a moment. "We could dump them in the river, but that might be too risky, too."

"Yeah, and we can't do that in broad daylight anyway," Josh replied. "Maybe we could throw them down that old well by the foundry. They'd never get out of there."

"We'd have to wait until after dark to do that for sure," Gus added. "No, once we get that money I want to get out of here before noon. Let's just tie 'em up and get on over to that boarding house."

"We don't have any rope, Gus!"

"Well, tear up the bed sheets into strips. We can tie 'em with that…"

Josh tried to rip up the bed sheets, but the sheets wouldn't tear.

"Use your knife, you idiot," Gus yelled.

Suddenly there was a loud knock at the door. Josh glanced at Gus. "Don't say anything!" He whispered hoarsely.

"Open the door! This is the police! Open up, we have a report of a disturbance in this room! Open this door now!"

"Out the window! Quick!" Josh said.

Gus slid the window open and both men jumped down to the ground. Gus ran off to get the money, but Josh hurt his leg and limped away towards a wooded area nearby.

The police kicked in the door and burst into the room, guns drawn. They looked at us; we were bruised, bleeding and in desperate need of immediate help.

One of the officers laughed. "Oh, just what I thought. Just a couple of soiled ladies that got smacked around by some of their clients. Should we arrest them, sarge?"

"Yeah, let them spend a little time in the jail house. It'll set "em straight and learn them a lesson."

"We are not prostitutes!" I cried.

"Yeah, sure ya' aint!" Laughed the sarge. "We get them here all the time…"

Nellie Belle and I were handcuffed and taken to the town jail. We did not have the strength to resist.

It was a filthy jail cell and smelled of urine. I became nauseated and vomited several times. Nellie Belle looked horrid. Her face was swollen something terrible.

We were lucky. There was a brawl outside a gaming room around eight o'clock that evening and several men were arrested. They released us to make room for these new arrivals.

We rushed to the Frontier Inn and knocked on the door of the room. Katherine opened the door and screamed when she saw us. Pelina made us lay down and she and Katherine put cool wet towels on our faces. This relieved the pain and helped to bring down the swelling after several hours.

When I was feeling better, I told Pelina and Katherine what had happened.

"You are both lucky to be alive," Katherine told us. "These are extremely violent men to beat women like that."

Pelina looked angry. "Ginny, let's go speak to Mr. Wrampelmeier about your mistreatment by those rotten policemen. They need to be reprimanded."

"I agree, Pelina. We will talk to them at breakfast tomorrow morning."

We met the Wrampelmeier's in the hotel lobby when it was time for breakfast. They were both livid when they saw Nellie Belle and me. Our faces were still a little swollen and bruised.

I told them about all the events of the previous evening as we walked to the hotel restaurant and were seated. I described how Flynt was killed and sarge wounded. As I told them how Nellie Belle and I were assaulted by Gus and Josh, they shook their heads in disbelief. Then when I told them how the policemen had arrested us at the hotel and accused us of being prostitutes, Mr. Wrampelmeier's face became red." This is inexcusable!" He exclaimed in disdain. "I will talk to the police inspector immediately and have these officers disciplined. They truly do not belong on the police force."

"This is all so completely deplorable, "Mrs. Wrampelmeier said. "This nonsense needs to end now."

"Let's hope so, dear. Hopefully it's almost over," Mr Wrampelmeier said as he took a sip of his coffee. "Ginny, have you found out any information about the wounded man, sarge? Is he expected to recover?"

"We don't know yet. He's probably still at the hospital," I replied.

After breakfast we went to the hospital to inquire about sarge. We sat on a bench in the waiting room for a long time. A doctor came out and told us that the sarge was not expected to make it. I asked to be notified immediately about his condition.

We returned to our room. Later that afternoon the hospital sent a message to our hotel informing us that the sarge had expired.

The man who murdered my parents so brutally five years ago was now dead. I became silent when I learned the news. I brushed tears from my eyes. I would never forgive and forget what these evil men had done, and the truth of the Biblical verse "He who lives by the sword shall perish by the sword" and "vengeance shall be mine" now took on a whole new meaning. This was my vindication. It was a bittersweet victory in every way, but even so, it would not bring my parents back.

Pelina and Katherine were a great comfort in this time of desperation, and they helped me to find hope. They also provided support for Nellie Belle. I was fortunate to have them at my side at a time like this.

There was a knock at the door. I was afraid to open it. What if it were Gus and Josh come back to finish us all off?

Katherine went to the door.

"Who is it?" She politely asked.

"This is Major Nate Parker from the Newport Army Barracks. I am here to investigate the report that you made to our department headquarters."

Katherine opened the door. A clean-shaven gentleman wearing a blue army uniform with two rows of shiny brass buttons on the front was standing there holding his officer's hat at his side. He had sandy, wavy hair and blue eyes. I think that Nellie Belle fell in love with him at first sight.

"Oh, please do come in. I have always loved men in uniform," she smiled.

It was good to see Nellie Belle getting back to her old self again.

"I am here concerning the report filed on Wednesday," he said as he entered the room. "Who is Miss Ginny Chamberlain?"

"I am Ginny." I came forward and he took my hand gently in his and smiled. Nellie Belle appeared to be envious.

He looked at my face and then at Nellie Belle. "Looks like both of you have been in a fist fight," he said jokingly.

"Well, it's a long story, sir," I said.

"I will ask you about that later then," he said.

We all sat down at the window table and discussed my written report. He took it from his leather side bag and placed it on the table.

Major Parker looked at me intently. "Ginny, could you please tell me what you are doing here in Newport?"

I recounted my entire story beginning with my parents murder and then explained our reasons for coming to Newport.

He looked with conviction into my eyes. "This was a terrible ordeal for you, Ginny, especially at such a young age. I am truly sorry for this violent deed that has caused all of this suffering and hardship. Two of those men that you described to me and mentioned in your report are now dead…Flynt Conner and Sergeant Bolin."

"Yes, we know that they are both deceased," I replied. "It happened last night in front of McCoy's Tavern on Monmouth Street."

"Exactly. And that brings us back to the investigation. Your report mentions that there were stolen goods that had been pillaged from some wealthy estates during the invasion of the South. How did you learn of this activity?"

"We eavesdropped on their conversations at their hotel room in Louisville. They openly bragged about plundering Southern plantation houses. Sarge told the men that he was bringing the stolen goods up to Newport from Frankfort and that they were going to be rich men."

The Major nodded and glanced down at my written report. "You mention a freight wagon here in the documentation. We have determined that this freight wagon belongs to a foundry near the Ohio River. The information which you provided in your statements has helped us to launch a large-scale investigation. We do not condone this conduct in the army and it is a violation of our protocols."

I nodded in affirmation of this promising news. A wonderful feeling crept through my body, finally my efforts were reaping results.

"I hope that this will put an end to this sort of thing," I said.

Major Parker smiled at me. "We are making headway now, thanks in large part to your report." He looked out the window a moment and seemed to be remembering something that troubled him.

"Many field commanders turned their heads to this rampant foraging by wanton soldiers during the Civil War. Believe it or not, some of these commanders were "on the take." They openly denounced pillaging, but secretly allowed it as long as they got their share of the take. Towards the end of the war things became very ugly during Sherman's march. I'm sure you all know about that; the burning of Atlanta and Sherman's march to the sea. The land was scorched from Atlanta to Savannah, and onwards into South Carolina. Civilians were woefully mistreated, and the soldiers came to be called bummers, their purpose being solely to strike terror into the population, and to exact retribution on them. This was a very dark time in our history. Men like Sargent Bolin and Flynt Cain were very much involved in this looting, and it seems that they have held onto their loot, waiting for the right moment to get the most money for it. There is a hiding place somewhere out there where all this stolen property is being stored. We hope to find out where it is."

Major Parker looked at me and Nellie Belle. "Please tell me about this bruising on your faces, Ginny and…."

"Nellie Belle. I was with Flynt when he was shot down by sarge last night"

The major nodded. "I see…and then what happened?"

"Ginny stayed the night with me at my hotel room. In the morning Gus and Josh, two of the men that knew sarge, burst into my room and demanded money. When I told them that we did not have it, they beat us senseless. The police came and then the men ran off. They found Flynt's address that I had written on a slip of paper in my purse. They were going to break into his room and take the money."

"Nellie Belle, would you mind writing all of this down in a statement as a separate report? I know these men and they will be disciplined."

"I don't write so well," Nellie Belle replied. "Can Ginny do it for me?"

"Sure, Ginny can do it as long as you sign it with a witness."

Major Parker assured us that there would be a thorough investigation and that the army would take action to stop the sale of stolen property pillaged during the Civil War. These men would be "weeded" out of the service, he said.

The next day police were summoned to a Cincinnati hotel to quell a disturbance. Two men were fighting over money. When Major Parker got wind of it he sent two army police officers to investigate.

The Cincinnati police found Josh dead in a pool of blood. Gus had escaped and was reported leaving the city headed towards Chillicothe. The army and police lost his trail.

A few days later I purchased a copy of the Cincinnati Enquirer as we waited at the train station for our trip home. A headline on the second page announced:

Soldier Found Dead

Yesterday a soldier was found dead near Paint Creek in Ross County. He had suffered injury to the head and torso. The cause of death and the soldier's identity is unknown.

It was a brief article, but I was sure that the unknown soldier was Gus. He probably was killed for that dirty money. It seemed like that money had become a curse of death. I folded the newspaper and placed it in my handbag.

We boarded our train and headed out of Covington for our return trip back to Louisville.

Decisions

Back in Louisville Nellie Belle caught the first riverboat out of town to St. Louis and Memphis. I never saw her again.

I returned to my hotel room. Pelina and Katherine went home. I was very lonely by myself. I wrote in my journal the entire day, hoping that Walter would be back soon.

July 16, 1867

Walter is back today. I am so happy! He brought me gifts from the great city of New Orleans. A silver necklace and a diamond pendant. Tonight, we will go out for diner, afterwards, dancing.

July 17, 1867

Last night was fun, we had a delicious meal in a pub. The roasted beef there was excellent. While we were eating a man in shabby clothing came up to Walter and said, "You owe me, where's my money!" Walter excused himself from the table and talked to the man outside the restaurant. When he returned I asked him who that man was. He smiled and said that it was nothing, just an old acquaintance asking for money.

Walter's riverboat was going out of service for the year, it needed maintenance repairs. I was not at all disappointed to learn of this; now Walter would be with me and away from the river.

It was good waking up in the morning with Walter next to me. I got up and poured water from the pitcher into the wash bowl. I bathed standing on a floor mat with the perfumed soap I had bought in Cincinnati. I put on lotion, wet my hair, combed it, and put on a leisure dress.

Walter ordered room service. There was a knock at the door. Walter sprang from bed, donned a bath robe and opened the door. A scrumptious breakfast awaited us all finely laid out on a rolling cart.

Living in a hotel room had its benefits, not to mention the service and comfort. But I became uncomfortable in the fact that Walter and I were not married. Sure, there were plenty of women that slept around town, but I was not like that. I was not some saloon girl, out for thrills. I wanted a relationship and family. I continued to prod Walter for marriage.

Most people at the hotel assumed that Walter and I were married, at least that is what I hoped. To maintain respectability was important for a lady. I needed some assurance from Walter.

"Don't worry, Ginny, we will be married soon! You are my only girl!" He would say. A week later I was wearing a diamond engagement ring. Then I used some money that Walter had given me to buy a wedding dress.

September 12, 1870

I was the maid of honor at Pelina's wedding today. I was so happy for her. It was such a beautiful wedding, and I cried. She will always be my best friend. The wedding and reception lasted into the evening. I was angry that Walter did not attend.

When I returned to my room I wrote in my journal for a while, then I closed it and shut my eyes. I had not seen Walter since this morning. He said that he was going to visit with some friends at the wharfs. I was feeling shaken because of what had just happened.

I had returned from the wedding and was walking through the hotel lobby towards the stairs when this insane man ran up to me yelling "yer gonna pay for this wench!" Then he ripped the right sleeve completely off my best dress. I screamed and slapped the man. It took several men to get him away from me.

By ten pm Walter still had not returned to the room. I had a bad feeling that something was wrong. I decided to go out and look for him. I left the hotel and walked up Main to Fourth Street. I thought that Walter might be in one of the taverns. I noticed some men shouting over a card game in Dandy's. One of the men was Walter.

Now I knew how Walter was getting so much money. This was how he could afford our hotel room, the diamond jewelry, the fancy restaurants. He was a high stakes gambler, apparently a good one at that.

I must say that I was devastated by this turn of events. I had suspicions that something was going on all along. I recalled the conversation with the woman in the restaurant. So, this is what she meant when she said that Walter must be doing "something else". Then there was this insane man who ripped my dress. Was he one of the men that Walter had angered at a card game?

I returned to my hotel room and cried myself to sleep. It was late when Walter returned.

The next day after breakfast Walter left to get supplies at the dry goods store. When he returned he was furious.

He had found out about the insane man who had ripped my dress. I had never seen him so angry. He grabbed his gun and stormed towards the door.

"Any man that lays a hand on my woman will pay for it!" He shouted.

I tried to stop him. "Walter! No, please! I'm okay, he did not harm me!"

"He's gonna pay for this!"

He left in a rage, confronted the man, shot and killed him. Then he was gunned down by the man's brother. Walter died that night.

Time would not allow me to forget Walter. Not a day went by without Walter in my thoughts. The pain and sorrow were deep, like a knife in my heart. That pain of complete loss had devastated me once again, my parents taken from me at such an early age in a horrific way, and now the only man I loved. Once again, I withdrew into a world of solitude.

I was running out of money fast. Walter was no longer there to support me. I had to find work.

I found a job at the Wrampelmeier's furniture store. I was hired almost immediately at the showroom on Fourth Street. It was a privilege to work there selling such fine quality furniture. Mrs. Wrampelmeier was in charge. She ran a well-oiled machine and she was treated like a queen. I enjoyed my job. It was fun working with Mrs. Wrampelmeier, she was always pleasant and full of stimulating conversation. It was a family owned business and I was treated like family, too. They always invited me for Sunday dinner and special holiday meals. They were good people.

The Summer of 1877

One day as I went on my afternoon stroll, I walked by the orphanage. I stopped and stared at it. My eyes scanned the imposing brick building. It looked like a fortress with all my memories etched there within its walls. Tears streamed down my cheeks.

"Are you okay, Miss?" An old gentleman said.

"Yes, yes, I'm fine, thank you, kind sir."

I visited Katherine. She married and had children. She lived in a nice two-story house on Chestnut Street. I felt much better after my visit.

We continued to keep in touch and got together with Pelina often.

I still lived at the hotel. The rents there had fallen as it had become somewhat run down over time. I lived alone, and I did not marry.

October 1883

Pelina became very ill in the autumn of 1883. I took care of her two girls when she was in the hospital. They were quite a handful, running, yelling, bouncing on the beds. I was afraid that they would get me kicked out of the hotel. We spent many hours at the park running off all that excess energy. The girls stayed with me until the spring. I must say that I did enjoy their company, and I always looked forward to their visits whenever Pelina came to town.

I did not want to stay at the hotel any longer. In the fall I moved into a small white wood frame house on 7th Street. I liked that house very much and it was a short walk to my job at the furniture store.

My uncle died in 1885. He willed the farm to me. Not long after he died it fell apart. I was not able to maintain it because of my job. I was working every day at the furniture showroom.

Pelina fell ill again in the spring of 1889. I took care of her two lovely daughters during this time. Pelina went into the hospital and thereafter she took a turn for the worse. This was distressing to watch my best friend in such condition. She passed away the first week of May. I promised that I would take her daughters as there was not a stable home for them with their father, and he agreed with these arrangements.

Pelina's two daughters, Sara and Kate, became my legal stepdaughters. Sara was seventeen and Kate was fifteen. I loved them both dearly like my own girls. They both married and moved away in their 20th year.

In 1895, the furniture factory closed permanently. Mrs. Wrampelmeier became seriously ill and they moved to San Diego to be with family. She died the following year. I missed them very much, and the closure of the furniture factory was a great loss for Louisville.

Kate's marriage did not last long. She left her abusive husband and moved back in with me in 1897. We both lived together in the small white wood frame house on 7th Street. She worked as a waitress.

Kate had two children, Grace, born in 1895, and Clara, born in 1896. They were adorable! They always called me their "Granny".

In 1901 I visited the farm for the first time in many years. The house was gone except for the chimney and one wall. The land was overgrown with weeds.

I decided to invest my time and money into fixing up the farm house. I had the house rebuilt, keeping the old chimney and fireplace. It took the workers about five months to construct a new two story wooden frame farm house on the old foundation. I used it as a summer house for several years.

I moved back to the farm to live there permanently in 1910. I bought several horses. Kate continued to live in Louisville, but she and her children visited the farm almost every weekend. Clara especially loved the horses and goats.

June 17, 1917

I came to visit Clara today at her new house on Story Avenue. Kate was there also, Clara's husband and their two children.

After lunch I decided to go for a walk to visit all the places that I remembered from my youth.

I saw the hotel where I had lived for many years. It was abandoned, and it had been wrecked by vandalism. The front lobby was dirty and covered in cob webs. I was the only one there. I walked up the stairs to the second-floor parlor. There was broken glass everywhere and debris strewn about the floor.

The hotel was in shambles. Something attracted my attention to a pile of trash on the floor. Could it be? No, was this possible? I picked up a book with a tattered tan leather cover. I opened it. There on the inside cover, about half way down, I saw my name written in cursive handwriting.

Ginny

It was my long-lost journal. I wiped off the cover and skimmed through some of the pages.

On the walls, I saw the old tattered portraits. But the portraits were not as they once were. They were faded and peeling. I saw Union soldiers in dark blue uniforms in each one. Sarge, Flynt, Gus and Josh. They had blindfolds over their eyes, as though they were about to face the firing squad. I sensed the shame and guilt in every face. They paid for their crime. Yes, they paid.

It was getting late. The storm had passed but I still had no lights. I closed Ginny's journal. I thought of the old farm house on Mint Spring. My Grandmother (Clara) had sold it many years ago and it was no longer in our family.

I thought about the old trunks my mother and I had found in my Grandmother's house on Story Avenue. Those trunks were in an upstairs closet in my house now. That edition of the Cincinnati Enquirer from July 16, 1867 was still in one of the trunks. The gun was also still there, and Ginny's wedding dress which she never wore.

I looked at my watch. It was half past twelve. I walked slowly down the hall with Muffin at my side, carrying the hurricane lantern. As I opened my bedroom door I felt a cold draft of air on my face. Muffin growled. I shivered.

I would throw an extra blanket on the bed to keep warm on this chilly Kentucky night.

Made in United States
Orlando, FL
03 May 2024

46475851R10083